Tuesday, September 4

What a way to ruin a perfectly good summer—school. And as usual, the first day was a TOTAL DISASTER! Summer was way too short.

Why me? Why always me? I know the whole story is going to be all over school tomorrow. You watch. I'll be branded for life as the "little seventh grade kid who got stuffed in his locker." And then everyone will have to try it at least once. It will be the new sport at Filmore Junior High—"Who can shove little Dean Matthews in his locker the most times," with a special award for anyone who can keep him in there for a whole day. And I'm sure I'll have a whole section of the yearbook so that no one ever forgets. I hate school and I hate being a seventh grader! I hate being a little shrimpy seventh grader!

I can't believe
I have to do this

I can't believe
I have to do this

Jan Alford

Penguin Putnam Books for Young Readers

Copyright © 1997 by Jan Alford. All rights reserved.
This book, or parts thereof, may not be reproduced in any form
without permission in writing from the publisher.
A PaperStar Book, published in 1999 by Penguin Putnam Books for Young Readers,
345 Hudson Street, New York, NY 10014.
PaperStar is a registered trademark of The Putnam Berkley Group, Inc.
The PaperStar logo is a trademark of The Putnam Berkley Group, Inc.
Originally published in 1997 by G. P. Putnam's Sons.
Published simultaneously in Canada. Printed in the United States of America.
Library of Congress Cataloging-in-Publication Data
Alford, Jan. I can't believe I have to do this / Jan Alford.   p.   cm.
Summary: Twelve-year-old Dean Matthews receives a journal as a birthday
present from his mother and records the events of the following year.
[1. Family life—Fiction. 2. Peer pressure—Fiction. 3. Schools—Fiction.
4. Diaries—Fiction.] I. Title.   PZ7.A38425Iaag   1997   [Fic]—dc20
96-43543   CIP   AC   ISBN 0-698-11785-9
10   9   8   7   6   5   4   3   2   1

*This book is lovingly dedicated to
Adrian
also known as "Dean"
and the rest of my wonderful family,
without whom I would have no inspiration.*

Contents

I can't believe
I have to do this

1

It Starts

I can't believe I have to do this! I can't believe she's making me do this. What is she trying to prove? She's lost her mind. She hates me. Maybe it's just a sick joke. I can't believe I have to do this!

My birthday. It's supposed to be the best day of the whole year, except for maybe Christmas. No, I take that back. *This* is supposed to be the best day of the year 'cause I'm the only one getting presents! And what did I get from a certain female parent? A journal. A journal?! Even the mountain bike Dad gave me doesn't make up for a stupid present like a journal. I don't remember asking for one. It never happened. But mothers always give you things you never ask for—things like underwear, Sunday shirts, ties, *and books*.

I could kinda tell from the wrapping that it was a book (Mom has this thing about reading), but I never expected a journal. All I could do was look at her and think, "She's gone nuts!" I mean it's bad enough to get a book you have to read, but a book you have to *write* in? Come on.

I guess Mom could tell what I was thinking so she *tried* to explain by saying it would be "good for me and teach me some discipline." As she was blabbering on and on about how her mother made her keep a journal and she learned to love it and it changed her life and blah, blah, blah, I finally figured it out—this is all because of the two C's I got on my report card last semester. She went ballistic when she saw them. I know she's still a little upset about it but I thought she understood. I was only missing a few assignments, and I wasn't really missing them. I had done them. I just kinda forgot to turn them in.

"Are you listening to me?" Suddenly I was back in the real world, with my mom and the journal. "I want you to write in it at least once a week for a year." (What?) And then she said (get this), "I bet by the end of the year you'll thank me."

(Yeah right! Keep dreaming, Mom!)

At least the rest of the day wasn't a total loss. Mom said I could invite Aaron over and we could do *anything* we wanted. So Aaron, Dad, and I went four-wheeling up in the foothills. It was great! We spent the whole day going everywhere normal people can't go. Dad's truck is just too cool. It'll go anywhere, up steep rock hills that scare you to death, through streams, into canyons that don't have real roads, and—the very best—through mud. Of course, that meant we had to wash and detail the truck big time when we got back to town, but even that was fun with Dad and Aaron. Then Dad took us to Telly's Pizza Place, which is just about the very best place you can go on your birthday (or *any* day). They make pretty good pizzas but that's not why I like to go. The best things about Telly's are the video games and the gyrosphere.

I'm not bragging or anything, but I'm a master at video games. I can beat Dad, I can beat Wyatt, I can beat any of the kids at school, and I can even beat Aaron (it's about the only thing I can beat him at). And for us game masters who demand the best in video games, there's absolutely no place like Telly's. They have every video game in the world. That's my dream. To have a basement as big as Telly's, full of arcade games.

But the best part of the whole day was when we made Dad ride the gyrosphere. It's pretty spooky the first time someone talks you into doing it. They strap you in, all spread-eagled, and then you get spun around and around and around until you don't know which way is up or which planet you're on. We kinda accidently (on purpose) forgot to tell Dad the most important thing about the gyrosphere— it's better to eat *after* you ride it, not before. I wished I had a video camera! He looked like he was gonna throw up, explode, and pass out, all at the same time. But he laughed (*after* he got off) and said, "Thanks, boys. I won't forget this one." Then he staggered back to the table. (He's getting old.)

After we dropped Aaron off and got back home, I asked Dad if he wanted to play the video game Aaron and his parents gave me. But before he could say anything, Mom butted in, "Don't you think *now* would be a good time to get started writing in your journal?"

"On my birthday?! This is a joke, right?" But she didn't look like she was joking. So I told her I didn't have anything to write about, so she just smiled her silly smile and said I should write about me and where I live and things I like to do. I looked at Dad like "Help!" but he just shrugged his shoulders and said, "Go on, we can play later." (Way to bail, Dad.)

I can't believe this! I'm just a twelve-year-old kid in sixth grade. I'm no writer. I'm no genius. I'm not a super athlete. I don't do anything special (except beat Dad and Aaron at video games). There is absolutely nothing to write about. I'm just a kid.

Saturday, April 7 (my birthday)

My name is Dean Matthews. I'm twelve years old. I'm in the sixth grade. I'm short. I weigh sixty-eight pounds. I have blond curly hair and blue eyes. I'm named after my dad's older brother, my uncle Dean, who I've never met because he died when Dad was just thirteen. He died in some kind of car accident. I've seen pictures of him and I don't look much like him. I guess Dad just liked the name. I live in Fillmore.

Actually, where we live is pretty cool. It's mostly desert and hot or at least warm all year long. No snow, no cold weather, and not much rain except sometimes we get great thunderstorms in the summer, like one last year. Me and Aaron were out in the desert building a fort when it hit. It was great! We sat in the fort and watched the lightning fill up the whole sky. It was so awesome. The thunder made the ground shake, kinda like an earthquake. Then the rain hit. I thought for a minute it would flatten the fort, but Aaron said, "You worry too much," and as usual he was right. We must be pretty good builders 'cause it held up and we only had one major leak. By the time we got home we were covered in mud. It was great! Until Mom saw us. She blew a gasket. First yelling because we tracked mud in the house, then because *we* were covered in mud, then because we were out in the desert during a thunderstorm. Then she was yelling just to yell. But it was still great.

■ · ·

I like to ride bikes, go hiking in the desert, play video games, go swimming, hang out with Aaron, go for walks with Thunder, and go to Telly's Pizza Place.

• • •

I just read back through my very first journal entry. Do I lead an exciting life or what? (This is a joke.)

2

The Family

This journal writing is getting real old. Mom's always asking if I've written but I never know what to write. A couple of days ago I tried to discuss it with her. All I said was, "This is a really dumb idea," and she came unglued! She said she didn't care what I thought. "I'm really getting tired of your attitude and all your complaining." (I don't complain that much.) "You're doing it and that's that!!" (Whoa, Mom, time to cut down on the caffeine.)

Well, so much for the direct approach. It was definitely time for another plan, so I was the perfect child for a couple of days. You know, trying to get on her good side and all. She was in a better mood today, so I decided to try (again) to discuss this little project of hers. After all, she always says we can "discuss anything." This time I tried real hard to avoid the word "dumb." I explained the reason I didn't like to write is because the things I write are d . . . uh . . . stupid. (She didn't like that word either.) So I hurried and said, "I'm just not a writer. The things I write sound weird and I'm not doing a very good job and . . . and . . . I feel like I'm a failure." And I tried to look real pathetic. I thought for sure that would get to her and she'd say, "You're right. You've given it a good try and you don't have to do it anymore."

Well, she didn't say what she should have. Instead she got that look on her face like she wasn't going to listen to *anything* I had to say *and* she turned her back on me. So I said, "Fine, you tell me what to write then." Big mistake! She had a real scary smile on her face when she turned back around. "Why don't you write about your family?"

Excuse me? My family? My "oh-so-exciting" family? (I should've kept my mouth shut.)

Saturday, April 28

My dad is a pilot. He's thirty-six. My mom is short. She's thirty-two and pregnant! My sister is Chelsea. She is eight. She's dumb most of the time. My brother, Wyatt, is six. He's in first grade and he's a big pest. This is my family.

After I got through, I thought, "Hey, this journal writing ain't so bad." I was feeling pretty good when I showed my masterpiece to Mom. She read it and started shaking her head.

What?

Then she said, "These are real people you're writing about. Important people. They're your family. Don't you have a few more thoughts and feelings about them?" (I didn't dare tell her what my thoughts and feelings were.)

Then she handed me my journal and said, "Try again, dear!" She said a *paragraph* about each person would be "appropriate." I tried to tell her our family just isn't that interesting. So she said, "Go into a lot of detail about us and include your favorite thing about each person."

This is ridiculous!!

Saturday, April 28 (again!)

My dad is a pilot. He's captain on a 737. He's tall and has dark brown hair and blue eyes. He likes to play with us and roughhouse and we have a lot of fun until Mom comes in and yells at everyone. He's gone on trips for six or seven days, but then he's home for four or five. My fa-

vorite thing to do with Dad is to go out in the truck and go four-wheeling. Another thing about Dad is he never gets mad.

Well, most of the time. There was one time when I was just looking through his closet and found this really cool jacket. It was blue and gold and had a big letter *F* on it and a whole bunch of pins and emblems that looked like footballs and basketballs and stuff. I was trying it on when Dad walked in. He totally exploded! He yelled the loudest I've ever heard him, **"Get out of here and NEVER TOUCH MY THINGS AGAIN!"** It was so weird. I've never seen him wear it. Anyway, most of the time he's pretty cool . . . unlike certain other people in the family. Which brings me to Mom.

. . .

Mom has curly brown hair and brown eyes. She's short and pregnant. She's the manager of an art gallery. My favorite thing about Mom is she likes to eat out better than stay home and cook. She yells sometimes, especially about our rooms not being clean and tidy. But mostly she just smiles a stupid smile while she makes us do things we don't want to do. Sometimes she's easy to talk to but other times she just won't listen or be reasonable. She has a great laugh (when she uses it).

My sister is eight. Her name is Chelsea. She has light

brown curly hair and brown eyes like Mom. She thinks she's sooo cute, but she's really a pain in the you-know-what. The worst thing about Chelsea is she's a big, fat tat-tletale. I don't have a favorite thing about Chelsea, except for maybe when she's at her friend's house.

My little brother is six and looks a lot like me. His name is Wyatt. His hair is blond and his eyes are blue. I guess he's OK, for a little brother. He does a lot of things that get him into trouble because, Mom says, he doesn't think be-fore he acts.

. . .

Like one time he got in trouble and Mom made him go in her room and sit on her bed for an hour. It's called a "time out." He went in her room and everything was quiet and peaceful. After an hour, Mom went in to finish talking to him and tell him he could come out. All of a sudden I heard her yell, **"Oh, Wyatt! What have you done?"** Well, I guess he got bored just sitting on her bed so he decided to "fix" her clock radio. He found a screwdriver, pliers, and wire cutters in Dad's nightstand and had kinda destroyed the whole thing. There were parts of this fancy clock all over Mom's bed. The radio knobs had been pulled off, the tape from the answering machine was all over the floor, the in-side workings were everywhere, the phone cord had been cut, and there he was, just sitting there—with the tools and the parts and a stupid grin on his face.

I felt kinda sorry for the kid after I got a look at Mom's face. He was going to get it big time! First she started yelling at him about leaving things alone that didn't belong to him. Then she put her hands on her hips and said, "What on earth did you think you were doing?" He just looked at her and said, "It wasn't working right, Mom, so I'm fixing it. Don't worry, I almost got it all back together." I just knew Mom was going to explode all over the room. But instead, she started laughing! She was laughing so hard she had tears in her eyes and she couldn't breathe. Then she hugged him! I couldn't believe it. I heard her tell Dad later, "Wyatt looked so sweet and innocent sitting in the middle of the bed with parts of the clock radio all around him. And he was so serious when he told me he almost had it all back together, I couldn't punish him. After all, he's just curious. Who knows, maybe he'll be the next Edison."

I wonder if that would work for me the next time I get into trouble? I mean, I can look sweet and innocent if I want. (Yeah right.)

· · ·

I have a dog named Thunder. He's a golden retriever and my best nonhuman friend. Thunder always likes me and never gets mad at me. He's probably the only one in the family who understands me.

I don't know if anyone else would consider Señora Ana a member of the family, but I do. She's been with us since

I was three or four. She's a Mexican lady who comes and takes care of us while Mom and Dad work. She practically runs our house. She helps us with homework and sometimes starts dinner for Mom. She laughs a lot, tries to teach us Spanish, and she hugs us real hard. She always smells like cookies and good stuff to eat. That's my favorite thing about Señora Ana.

. . .

I'm done! I wrote so much I have writer's cramp and a headache. I showed Mom how much I wrote and told her I needed some aspirin for the pain in my hand and my head but you know Mom—she just smiled that silly smile and said, "I think you'll live." But then she hugged(!!!) me and said, "You did a good job, kid. Keep it up." And then she added (you're not going to believe this), "Oh, by the way, Dean, you don't ever have to show me your journal. A journal is a very private thing. Everything you write is just between you and your journal."

I was so confused I started stammering, "But I thought . . . I mean you said I had to write in it once a week, and if you don't look at it, how will you know? I mean, I would do anything you told me to, but . . . uh . . . you don't want to see what I write?"

"Nope," she said, "if you can look me straight in the eye and tell me you've written in it at least once a week, I'll believe you and I'll never ask to see it ever." Then she added,

"It's a great way to yell at people without yelling at them, even your mom." Then she winked and walked off giggling to herself.

Now she tells me! Gee thanks, Mom. I can't believe her. All that writing for nothing.

3

Aaron

Saturday, May 12

This is the first time I've written anything in two weeks. It probably would have been longer, but I got caught by the "journal police."

Mom finally cornered me and asked how I was doing. (Oh, just great, Mom. I've always dreamed of spending the rest of my life writing in a journal.) I said, "Fine," and tried to look busy doing something—anything. Then she got specific. "Have you written in your journal this week?" I thought about lying but she can always tell when I fib. I stutter and turn red. It's real bad. So I just said, "Uh ... well ... not exactly." Then she asked why. I said, "Because I still don't know what to write. I can't write about my family every week. We're just not that interesting."

So she came up with another "great" idea. "Why don't you write about your best friend?" Then she added, "Think about it before you write. What makes you like him? Why are you best friends? You know, stuff like that."

(I gotta get a life!)

Of course, when I think about it, I could probably write a book about Aaron (except I'm not going to). He is so cool. He is definitely my best friend. We do everything together. We like the same things and we think the same way. We could be brothers, except we don't look anything alike. He has black hair and brown eyes and he's taller than me (but who isn't). He's also a lot stronger than me. He played grid-kid football last year and he was one of the best players. He rides the coolest mountain bike he got for his birthday, and he has a little bike he does tricks on. He's trying to teach me how to do some bike tricks like jumps and stuff, and I'm OK, but not near as good as Aaron. He's the best.

He's always in a good mood, and I can talk to him about anything. He always has the best ideas when we're bored. Like the time we dug a tunnel (or tried to) under his fence into the next yard. We probably would have made it except his dad made us stop because the fence started to sag. Then there was the time we made this huge spider web in my backyard. We strung it between the fence and the house and it covered the whole yard. We had to use all of Mom's white yarn and most of her black. You could tell she wasn't real thrilled about it (especially since we forgot to ask), but she said as long as we cleaned it up, it was OK. It looked so great, we didn't want to take it down, at least for a couple of days. We told everyone at school about it and a couple of the guys came home with us to see it. But Mom blew it. She had cut it up. All that was left were pieces of yarn all over the yard.

Sometimes Aaron and I go to the desert with our walkie-talkies and pretend we're in the army, fighting a war, or we're spies or things like that. Sometimes we take Thunder with us, but mostly we don't because he wants to chase rabbits and lizards, and it's hard to get him to come home. And then he gets burrs in his tail and sometimes cactus spines in his nose, or he'll chase and kill a lizard and bring it home. Then you should hear Mom yell, especially the time he put one on her bed because he was so proud of it. He was just giving her a present, but she didn't appreciate his offer and ended up yelling at me for letting him do it (like I can stop him or something).

I like staying at Aaron's house more than mine. His dad lets us stay up as late as we want and watch any movie we want, even real gross, bloody ones like *Zombie Massacre* or *Surfers from Hell*. Mom would just die, then ground me for life, if she knew I was watching "violent trash." I wish I could stay at Aaron's house all the time.

We really are best friends even though sometimes he

gets mad at me for no reason and won't talk to me. It never lasts very long though and then we're best friends again. Mom says that's just the way boys are. He even protected me once. That's how we met back in third grade.

I've always been the littlest kid in class. I'm not a wimp, but let's face it, I'm not going to win too many fights being a shrimp. Anyway, a bunch of us were on the playground after lunch. We were playing kickball when some big fifth graders decided to take our ball away. Now back in third grade I didn't have a lot of brains, so I ran after them and told them to give our ball back. (Yeah, like they were going to hand it right over.) They just laughed and walked away, so I ran up to the one with the ball and kicked him in the ankle. Real bad move! Before I knew it, he had me face-down on the ground telling me to "eat dirt" (like I had a choice). That's when I met Aaron. Actually, the first thing I met was his feet.

"Leave the kid alone!" It was Aaron. Well, since Aaron was only in third grade too, Godzilla wasn't in any hurry to let me up. I think he laughed. It was kind of hard to hear, you know, dirt in one ear, his knee in the other. Then Aaron said even louder, "Get off the kid. NOW!" That's when the fifth grader finally let me up (but he didn't let me go). He held me by my shirt collar and said, "Who's gonna make me?" Well, Aaron had got a whole bunch of other kids to stand beside him, just about every third and fourth grader on the playground. He said, "You might be able to beat up some of us, but not all of us. Let the kid go *now!*" Just then, a couple of teachers started to come out of the school, so the big kid let me go. But first he shoved me and I ended up back on the ground, and they still had our ball. (Life is never fair to the short and skinny.)

Anyway, Aaron helped me up and we've been best friends ever since. Since then we've talked about bullies and the day we met. I always figured he was real brave or had a death wish. But he said no. He was really scared too, but he hated seeing big kids pick on little kids.

Saturday, May 12

My best friend is Aaron Timmons. Everyone should have a friend like Aaron. He's the best. I think we'll probably be best friends forever.

4

The Informer

Why is it only me that gets in trouble? Chelsea and Wyatt do things that should get them in trouble, but everyone ends up thinking they're just so cute. I could puke!

Take for instance Chelsea, the tattletale. She tells on everyone about every little thing. You stick your tongue out and she tells. You eat downstairs in the family room and she tells. You break one little lamp and she tells. She gets everyone in trouble and everyone mad at each other. She's such a bad tattletale even Mom's fed up with her and told her if she tattles anymore, she'll get the same punishment as the person she tells on. You would think that would get her to shut up. Yeah right.

The other night when Mom and Dad were out, me and Wyatt got into a little fight. It wasn't that bad, except somehow I ended up kicking a hole (just a small one) in the wall. And that's when Chelsea started in about how she was going to tell and get me into a whole bunch of trouble. So I grabbed her by the shirt and said, "This time it was the wall. Next time it could be your face." It didn't even faze her. She just said she would tell and I would get into double trouble. I was ready to inflict serious pain when I remembered what Mom said, so I reminded her, you know, about telling and getting the same punishment. That shut her up (I thought). She didn't say another thing all night. I figured I finally had her right where I wanted her. I should've known better.

The next morning, Mom asked me to come into her bathroom so she could show me something. You know what Chelsea did? She drew a picture of the fight we had and titled it: *"Fight on Thursday. To Mom from Chelsea. Just a little note. P.S. If you look very closely, you will find a hole in the wall behind Dean's bedroom door. He did it. And he threatened to hurt me . . . BAD!"* And she had taped it to Mom's bathroom mirror. So then Mom asked me what I was going to do about the hole in the wall and why was I picking on Wyatt again and who did I think I was, threatening people. The whole thing was so unfair. I just had to ask, "Why isn't Chelsea getting in trouble too?"

"Well, Dean, technically she didn't tattle-tell. She tattle-*wrote*." And Mom started to laugh! She thought the note was funny and Chelsea didn't get in trouble at all. In fact, Dad called her a "smart little cutie." Well, I've got a news flash for all of them. Chelsea is definitely not cute. She's a royal pain in the you-know-what! And her day will come. In the meantime, I'm learning how to patch holes in the wall.

5

Mom to the Rescue

Thursday, May 24

Sometimes I think I have the best mom in the universe! She is so cool!

Last night Aaron and I were riding our bikes and these two big kids stopped us—Kent and Nick. They asked if they could ride our bikes and we said sure—just up the street and back. They rode around the block and didn't come back for a long time. When they did come back, we told them to give our bikes back but they said they were going to keep them. I yelled at them to give our bikes back and they tried to hit us. Aaron told me to go get his dad, and then he started running after them like he was going to fight them or something (he *does* have a death wish). They called us "babies," but they gave us our bikes back.

Later, they came back and told us to let them ride again. When we said no, they started after us. I got away, but they knocked Aaron down and started to take his bike. So I shouted, "I'm gonna call the cops!" They laughed and said they were just kidding. But before they left, they told us we better be careful, because we "never know what might happen," like a threat or something.

After I got home, I told Mom all about it. She flipped out! At first, I thought she was mad at me, but she wasn't. We got in the car and went over to Nick's house. Both of them were in Nick's garage. Mom stormed out of the car, slammed the car door (she kinda reminded me of a mother bear defending her cub), and the first thing she said was, "We can either talk out here and you *will* listen, or we can go inside and have this talk with your parents. Which would you prefer?" Nick said, "We can talk out here." (He looked so scared. It was great!) Kent started to leave but she said, "Oh, no, you're part of this too." He tried to be real cool. "You can't make me stay." So she took a step toward him and smiled her real scary smile that says, *"You don't even want to think about messing with me!"* (which I usually hate because it's aimed at me), and said, "OK, we'll see you *and* your parents later . . . at *your* house." He decided to stay.

Then she really let them have it. She told them they better stop picking on kids younger and littler. And that if she ever heard of one of them picking on me or *anyone* else again, she wouldn't just talk with their parents, she would bring the police in on it. She said, "I won't hesitate one minute to press charges." Nick started looking at Kent and kind of laughing and said, "Yeah right. What charges?" Mom got real serious and real close to his face and said in a real low voice, "Assault and battery, tough guy." That made him stop laughing real fast. Right before we left she looked them both right in the eye and pointed at them and said, "We do understand each other, don't we?" When they said yes, she said, "I hope so, because I promise you that if there is any more trouble, I will see to it that you both face the full consequences of your actions." (I love it when she talks like that. I don't always understand it, but I love it.) Then we left.

When we got home, I called Aaron and told him what Mom did. He said he told his dad what happened and his dad had said just to stay away from the big kids.

• • •

It was so strange, you know, to have my mom play Rambo like that. But it made me feel real good to have her stand up for me. She says she hopes she didn't embarrass me or make it bad for me around the neighborhood. I told her, "No way. It was great!" She worries over such silly things. And besides, if it does get bad, I'll just have her beat everyone up! She was GREAT!

6

Families

I don't think any mother who has a kid who's almost a teenager should get pregnant and have more babies. It's kind of embarrassing. I don't know what Mom and Dad were thinking about! Three kids are plenty (actually too many), but Mom said four will make everything even. You see, we found out Mom's going to have a baby girl.

Mom had a test done (because she's so old) to make sure the baby's all right. It's called an amino . . . ceesis (or something like that). Anyway, they can tell if the baby is going to be a girl or a boy, and we found out it's a girl. Chelsea's excited because she says she's always wanted a sister and that girls are better than boys. Señora Ana is excited because she *loves* to take care of babies. Yuck! Wyatt says he's happy because now Chelsea will have someone *else* to play with and won't bother us "guys" so much. Poor kid. He doesn't know what it's like to have a baby around. They can't play with you or talk to you or do anything except cry and eat and sleep. I know all about it because I was around when *both* Chelsea and Wyatt were born and they were both royal pains.

Mom's happy because she says it's fun to dress up little girls. And believe it or not, I think even Dad's excited about having a girl. He says it will be neat to have a "balanced" family, you know—two boys, two girls. Mom says it really wouldn't matter what it was, he just likes having babies around. I don't know. I think babies can be a mess (in more ways than one). But I guess they can be kinda cute sometimes, like when they're sleeping.

Anyway, they went on and on and *on* talking about babies until I was ready to throw up. Then Aaron called. He asked if I could spend the night, but Mom said no. She wanted me to spend the weekend around the house with the family. (Mom can be so stupid.) When I asked her why, she said, "Because it's family time." I told her I already had enough "family time" and "baby talk" to last ten years! Then she started blabbering about how "family is the only important thing" and "they're the only ones who will stick by you and always love you." I said, "I still don't understand why I can't have just *one* night with my friend." She got kinda irritated with me and said, "Because I said so, that's why."

That's when I made the *big* mistake. I just reminded her that she had always said she would always give me a *good* reason when she said no, "And I don't think *'Because I said so'* is a very good reason." I've *gotta* learn when to shut up. I thought she was going to have a stroke! She sent me to my room and told me I was grounded. (Hey . . . I thought that's what spending a weekend with my family was.)

And then today, Aaron called and told me how much fun he had with this kid Stach who just moved in next door to him. His real name is Anastacio because his dad is Italian, but they call him Stach for short. He's fourteen. They got to stay out real late and play basketball. Then Stach went and got some M-80 firecrackers and they went around the neighborhood putting them in people's mailboxes. Aaron said a couple of the mailboxes actually blew up!

Thanks to Mom I missed all the fun again. Family time. What a joke.

Sunday, June 3

Now I'm kind of glad I didn't spend the night at Aaron's house. Someone at one of the houses where Stach and

Aaron lit the M-80s called the cops. So the police were all over Aaron's neighborhood asking questions. Aaron was real scared but Stach said "no sweat" since no one saw them. I guess so. Except on TV, the cops always find out.

7

Disciplinary Paragraphs

Tuesday, June 5

I live in a prison!

First the journal (which is bad enough), and now I have to write a disciplinary paragraph. You see, in our house, if you break a rule (and you can read and write) Mom makes you write a paragraph about the house rule you broke, why she has the rule, and then you have to end the paragraph with a promise to do better. Mom says promises are harder to break if they're written down. Whatever.

But today was different. It was actually all Wyatt's fault. It started when we were playing video games and Wyatt wouldn't play right. He kept going back to the same spot over and over and over because he thought it was funny to see the monkey pound his chest. He was running out of time and he wouldn't listen when I told him to get moving. I guess my voice got kinda loud because Mom walked in and reminded me it was only a game and should be fun for everyone. But after she left, Wyatt *still* wouldn't play right. So, I grabbed the controller (just to get him going) and he started yelling. I got so fed up with him and the stupid way he plays the game, I kinda accidently threw the controller at him, and it kinda hit him on the nose, and of course, he started bawling. To make matters worse, his nose started bleeding (just a little), so he went screaming down the hall to Mom.

When Mom stormed into the family room, her face was all red (which happens when she's trying not to yell). She stood there for a minute just looking at me, like she was going to explode or something—then she let me have it. I got the full ten-minute lecture about house rules, respecting other people, importance of family, and "poor little Wyatt's feelings," *plus* I have to write the stupid disciplinary paragraph. What am I supposed to write: *"It was all Wyatt's fault"*? If I wrote that, I might end up never seeing the outside world again. So I wrote a very nice and humble paragraph about what a crud I am and finished by saying, "I promise I will not get so upset over the video games because when you do, it makes the whole family unhappy and games aren't fun anymore." I showed it to Mom and tried to look as sad and sorry as I could, but she wasn't buying it. So on top of everything else, she grounded me from the games for two weeks.

. . .

I live in a prison with no hope of parole.

8

School's Out

Saturday, June 9

School's out and I love it! No more homework. No more teachers preaching at me. No more getting up at the crack of dawn. No more school lunches!

Yesterday we had sixth grade graduation and Mom and Dad were there with the video camera. We had to march in (just like they do in high school) and go up and get our diplomas. Then after the principal finished his speech and said he wished us all good luck in junior high, everyone started cheering and clapping and yelling and stomping their feet and making a whole bunch of noise. It was great!

But the best part is, SCHOOL IS OUT FOR ALMOST

THREE WHOLE MONTHS! I'm going to have FUN, FUN, and more FUN. Aaron and I will ride bikes every day and swim and sleep over and sleep till noon and maybe go camping and fishing and not have to worry about if we got our homework done or if we're going to fail a test or "miss an assignment."

Last summer, we had the best time. Aaron's mom and dad were going to Disneyland and they invited me to go with them. Mom must have been having a REAL good day because she said yes. It was so cool. The first day we were there we got to the park early in the morning and rode every ride we could find. Even when we had to stand in super long lines, it was great, watching all the people (making fun of them) and getting excited for the ride. We watched the Light Parade and fireworks (which were better than any Fourth of July). The last ride we rode was at eleven o'clock at night! It was the biggest Ferris wheel I've ever seen. It was so neat up there, with all the lights and people and music. Then Aaron started swinging the chair real hard. It was scary, but so much fun. We started talking about what it would be like to have the Ferris wheel go berserk while we were on it. Aaron said when we grow up we ought to make a movie about kids getting stuck on a haunted Ferris wheel. By the time the ride was over, he had the whole story made up. His imagination is awesome. I wish I was more like him. The next day we went to the ocean and swam all day. Summers with Aaron are the best!

I wonder if Mom would give me the summer off from writing in my journal. Doesn't hurt to ask.

She said, "Keep dreaming."

But you know what's really weird? I don't even care, because . . .

. . .

SUMMER IS HERE!!!

9

A Taste of Freedom

Tuesday, June 19

My hair is so awesome! I was meant for this haircut. I look just way too cool.

It all started when Mom and I were having an argument (she calls them discussions) about how she treats me like a baby. Anyway, shock of all shocks, Mom *finally* agreed with me about something. After I picked myself up off the floor, she said she and Dad had been talking about it and they thought I should be allowed a little more freedom and make some decisions for myself, even if they don't always agree with me. (I wonder what book Mom's been reading this time?)

Anyway, I decided to try out this "make your own decision" thing, so I showed her a picture of how I want my hair. It's kind of radical, but I like it. It's really short on the sides—almost bald, but then you leave the top kinda long hanging over where it's cut on the sides. I could tell Mom didn't like it very much, *but* they let me do it. I got it cut yesterday. Even with all my curly hair, I look so cool. I wonder how far I can push this thing? I've always wanted an earring, just one, in my left ear. That would be super cool.

Then Aaron invited me to spend the night. I held my breath, said a little prayer, and asked Mom. I *cannot* figure her out. Most of the time when I ask to do something, she gives me the third degree, drags me over the coals, blabbers on and on about things I don't understand, then usually says no. But this time, she said *yes!*

We had so much fun! We played with some of his new video games, and after dinner we went out and played basketball with Stach.

Stach is pretty cool. He lives with his mom because his parents are divorced and his dad lives in New York. He doesn't have any brothers or sisters. (Neither does Aaron. They are so lucky not to have little kids around the house.) Stach dresses kinda like the bikers on TV, ripped-up jeans and cool T-shirts with sayings on them. His hair is kinda long and blond and he's taller than Aaron. He can do all kinds of tricks on a skateboard and really knows basketball! He beat me and Aaron together! He plays kinda rough (shoves and trips and elbows us) but he says, "Time to

grow up, boys. That's the way they do it in the big leagues."
Stach said we would have to go over to his house sometime
and have a party because his mom is gone a lot and no one
would be around to bother us.

Aaron was right. It's going to be fun having Stach
around.

10

Honesty Is
the Best Policy

Mom is starting to get real fat! Every time she looks in the mirror, she makes a face and says she's too old to be pregnant. I could've told her that before *she got that way. Wyatt always says, "You're not old, you're just pregnant." Then she laughs and hugs him. (Good one, Wyatt.)*

I guess she looks kinda cute and not as old as she is. She's thirty-two and that's pretty old. She sure doesn't act as old as she is sometimes. I catch her turning up the stereo once in a while and dancing around the house, singing with the music. Most of it's old-time music, but every now and then she'll turn on the good stuff. I guess she can be pretty cool once in a while. I can usually talk to her about anything, as long as I'm honest. She says it's real important to always be honest, even if you're in trouble, because that's how you earn respect and trust. She says as long as I'm honest, I won't get in as much trouble as if I lie. Boy, that's the truth!

Like last Halloween, I had to take Wyatt with me trick-or-treating even though me and Aaron had our own plans (if you know what I mean). I decided Wyatt would just have to join our kind of fun. We snuck a dozen eggs out of the fridge (Aaron got two dozen) and we threw them at houses and cars (and a few trick-or-treaters). I guess someone saw us, 'cause when we got home, there were Mom and Dad, waiting to jump down our throats. Well, *my* throat anyway. At the time, I didn't know Mom already knew what we had done. She took me into my room and Dad took Wyatt into the living room. When Mom asked if I had been out "egging" houses, I looked her straight in the eye and said, "No! I would never do that!" Then she said, "Are you *sure?* There have been some kids throwing eggs around the neighborhood and I want to make sure it wasn't you." So I looked real sincere and told her again that I would *never . . . ever* do *anything* like that. Then we all met in the living room. Dad looked pretty happy so I figured Wyatt must have kept his mouth shut and everything was OK. So then Mom asked Wyatt if he had fun trick-or-treating with me, and that's when it all fell apart.

He said, "It was great! I got lots of candy and Dean

showed me how to do the 'tricks' part." Mom looked so innocent and said, "Oh, what do you mean, Wyatt?" I could feel my face getting hotter and hotter and I was hoping Wyatt would have a convulsion and slip into a coma or something. Instead, he said, "We threw lots of eggs at people's mailboxes and I'm a real good thrower. Dean said so. I hit five mailboxes and one door. It was so much fun! Can we do it next year too?" (I couldn't even believe it. Little kids have absolutely no brains.)

Then Dad burst out laughing. I started thinking maybe things weren't so bad until I looked at Mom . . . and she wasn't laughing *at all.* Fire was shooting out of her eyes, so Dad hurried and said, "You know, dear, all young boys go through this. You can just expect it." So I looked at Mom to see if she would lighten up. (Yeah right.) She said, "I realize that, *however . . ."* (I hate that word) "I do not expect a son of mine to lie to me. That is never acceptable." Then she got real loud and ugly. "NOR WILL IT BE TOLERATED!" And she looked at me until I thought her eyes were going to pop out of her head. So guess who got grounded from friends, TV, and video games for two weeks? You guessed it . . . me and *only me.* All Wyatt had to do was apologize and clean some mailboxes (which I had to do too). So when Mom says, "You'll get into more trouble if you lie than if you confess," she isn't kidding.

So now sometimes I tell her about the things I do that aren't so cool. And sometimes, we have amnesty talks, where the things I tell her, I don't get into trouble for because I was honest and confessed. And she usually tries to keep her temper. She's even told me some dumb things she did when she was a kid. Like when she was ten and told her mom she was sick so she could stay home from school. She wanted to make Grandma think she had a bad fever so she put the thermometer on the heater in her room, then hurried and put it in her mouth when Grandma came to check her. She said Grandma looked pretty surprised when she saw Mom's fever was 112!

At the end of our talks, she always hugs me and tells me she loves me, even after the time I told her about yelling at Señora Ana and hurting her feelings. I guess I have a pretty cool mom (except when she's going ballistic).

11

When Sad Things Happen

Thursday, July 5

A really, really sad thing happened. It doesn't make any sense. I hate to see Mom cry.

Last week, Dad brought Mom home early from work and I could tell she had been crying. She went straight to her room without talking to anyone. Dad said she was going to sleep for a while and we should leave her alone. Then he left. That made me kind of scared. I thought maybe Mom and Dad were mad at each other and might get a divorce. Aaron was telling me how his parents used to fight a lot, his Mom would cry all the time, and they *almost* got a divorce. A lot of my friends' parents are divorced and I guess I started to think it was my turn. It didn't seem like Mom and Dad fought a lot, but I thought maybe they do it late at night when we're asleep.

When Dad came back he had a big bunch of flowers and a card. He called all us kids to come have a talk and told us the baby girl inside Mom had died. All I could say was, "How?" Dad said he didn't know. Him and Mom went to the doctor for a checkup and the doctor couldn't find the baby's heartbeat with his stethoscope so he sent them to get a test—an ultrasound—and it showed the baby's heart wasn't beating and that it was dead.

We were all so sad. Señora Ana started to cry and went to the kitchen. Chelsea and Wyatt were crying and I felt like crying but I didn't. We all signed the card and Dad said we would give it to Mom when she woke up.

Señora Ana fixed dinner and stayed around to help Chelsea with homework and give Wyatt a bath—the stuff Mom usually does. She was reading Chelsea and Wyatt a story when Mom finally came out of her bedroom. She still looked pregnant, but she said that's because the baby was still inside her and that she had to go to the hospital the next morning so she could deliver it. When she was trying to explain everything, she kept saying, "I lost the baby." So Chelsea finally said, "I don't understand. The baby died, right? So now she's in heaven, right? So she's not *lost*.

She's living with God." Mom started crying and I was ready to strangle Chelsea. But then Mom got a little smile on her face, hugged Chelsea real tight and said, "You're absolutely right, Chelsea. You are such a smart little girl."

The rest of the night Mom acted pretty normal. But later, after us kids went to bed, I heard her crying. I couldn't sleep, and I couldn't figure out why. I didn't really want another baby around the house, but I didn't want it to die!

• • •

I wonder why the baby died? Maybe Mom works too hard. Maybe she shouldn't be working at all. On TV they're always telling pregnant ladies to relax and not do too much and not have too much stress. Maybe it's not work. Maybe us kids are too much stress for her. She's always telling us we drive her crazy. I guess I feel kind of guilty about the whole thing, after all the things I thought about not liking babies and them being a real pain.

• • •

The next morning, before any of us kids got up, Mom went to the hospital. Dad went with her but came home late in the afternoon. He said Mom was doing OK and wanted us to have some fun since it was the Fourth of July. He asked who wanted to go see fireworks. Wyatt got all excited and said he wanted to go, so we went. While we were waiting for the fireworks, all I could think about was Mom in the hospital and being alone and sad and it made me feel real

47

bad. I asked Dad if we could go see her after the fireworks, but Dad said it would be too late. Then Wyatt said, "I want to go see Mommy." So Dad explained, "If we go see your mom, we'll have to miss the fireworks. We just can't do both. I'm sorry." All of a sudden Chelsea stood up and said, "We're going. I don't care what Wyatt and Dean want to do. We're going to see Mom." Then Wyatt said, "Yeah, I want to see Mommy. Don't you, Dean?" I was already folding up the blanket.

When we got to Mom's room, she was reading. She looked OK. Her stomach was a lot smaller and she was smiling and acting normal. She even joked with us about hospital food and getting a good rest away from us kids. There wasn't much to do so we watched TV. I don't think she was really as happy as she was acting because once when I looked over at her, she was looking at Dad and she had tears in her eyes, then Dad put his hand on her shoulder. It was a very sad Fourth of July.

When Mom came home today, she looked and acted like "good old Mom" but I didn't feel like "good old Dean." It still really bothered me about the baby dying. And finally, I figured it all out . . . it's God's fault.

So I asked Mom why God let the baby die when she wanted it so much. She said, "Oh, Dean, something went wrong inside of me and the baby just died. Even the doctor doesn't know why." I asked her if working so much made the baby die or if us kids stressing her out hurt the baby. She didn't answer me for a while and I thought she was going to cry again, but she finally said in a real soft, fuzzy voice, "No, it's not anyone's fault." She said at first she blamed herself, because she hadn't planned this baby and wasn't sure if she really wanted another one. (I couldn't believe it! Mom had kinda felt the same way about the baby I did.) But then she said, "I know deep in my heart that I didn't make the baby die. You kids didn't make the baby die. Me working didn't make the baby die. And, Dean, God didn't make the baby die. It just happens sometimes."

I had to ask, "So why didn't God *stop* the baby from dying?" She said, "It doesn't work that way." I got kinda mad then, at God, you know. "I don't think that's very fair. God can do anything He wants and He should have *stopped* the baby from dying because we're a good family and we would have loved it . . . her, even if we hadn't planned on another baby. And Dad had wanted another little girl . . . and . . . well, He just shouldn't let bad things happen to us. It's just not right and it's not fair!"

I should've known when to keep my mouth shut because then she started to cry again. And I felt like a jerk. She put her arm around me and said, "God loves us very much, but that doesn't mean He does everything *for* us. And I think He's very fair. After all, He gave me three of the best kids in the whole world." Then Mom gave me a big hug. That should've made me feel pretty good, but it made me feel like crying.

·   ·   ·

Mom looks so sad. I wish I could make everything all better for her.

12

A Most Awesome Experience

I can't believe what happened!! I think my parents are finally starting to get with the program! It's a real-life miracle and the most amazing thing that's ever happened to me.

I was going to write it all down in my journal, but there's way too much! It all started when I finally and truly decided that I wanted an earring in my left ear.

I practiced for two days in the mirror. I decided I would look Mom right in the eye and say, *"I think it's a decision I should be able to make for myself."* (Sound impressive?) *"I'm old enough! I decide what clothes I want to wear. I decided how I wanted my hair cut. This is really no different."* (Yeah right.)

So I got up all my courage and went to ask her. She was cleaning Chelsea's room (which was a total disaster as usual) and something told me it wasn't the right time. She was muttering things like, "These kids don't appreciate all they have," and "I'm going to give everything to the Salvation Army," and "Next time there won't be a Christmas, just a bunch of coal," and she was kinda throwing things around and had a wild look in her eye. So I turned around and slunk back to my room. Better to wait until her mood changed. While I waited, I cleaned my room.

The next day I woke up feeling great, feeling brave, feeling like I really had nothing to lose. So, I just did it. I told Mom I wanted to talk to her. She was doing the dishes and said, "Sure, go ahead." I told her I wanted her to sit down. She looked up real fast and real scared so I tried to laugh real casual-like and told her to relax (yeah right, and all the while I'm sweatin'). I thought about telling her I wanted something really weird like my nose pierced or a tattoo on my chest so that she wouldn't think one little earring was such a big deal. But I got too nervous.

"I've thought a lot about it and I've decided I really want to get an earring!"

She looked shocked, but she didn't explode. Then I hurried on, "Only my ear . . . only *one* ear!" Then she got that look on her face like she's probably going to say no. So I hurried on and reminded her about making some of my own decisions and being a big kid now and all that stuff. I thought if I could keep talking long enough, she wouldn't be able to say no. But then I ran out of words so I had to stop and just look at her. I was panting like I had just run a race and I could hear my heart beating in my ears. She didn't say anything for a long time. Then she stood up and went over to the sink and stood there for a *loooong* time. I couldn't tell if she'd forgotten she was talking to me or gone into a trance or what. Then she turned around and said, "You'll have to discuss it with Dad when he comes home on Friday. Whatever he decides, I'll go along with . . . *but*" (there's always a "but") "I want you to think about it some more and think about it *very, very* seriously."

She didn't fool me with this "think about it" thing. She had a plan. She was going to ambush Dad when he got home to tell him all about it before I could talk to him. Then when the answer was "No" it would be all *his* fault and not hers. What a hassle when you can't make your own decisions without getting approval from parents. Parents have totally too much control over their kids' lives.

Anyway, I knew I had to get to Dad first. As soon as he came home from his trip and walked in the house, I asked him if we could have a *private* talk. He asked if I could wait because he was kinda tired. I said, "Dad, this is *real* important! It's like important to my life!" So he kinda sighed and said, "OK. Come in the bedroom and let's get it over with." (Not a real good start.)

As soon as we got through the door, I just came out and said real fast, "I've thought a lot about it and I want an earring and I've already talked to Mom and I only want it in one ear and Mom said I would have to talk to you and it's not really such a big deal and Mom said whatever you decide she would go along with and she made me think a lot about it and I still want one and I think this is one of those decisions I should make for myself because I'm old enough and . . ." (I finally had to stop because I ran out of breath.)

First Dad started to laugh. Then when he saw I was serious, he stopped laughing real fast. He shook his head and rubbed his eyes like he does when he has a bad headache. I started to think I should have waited until he wasn't so tired. Then he asked, "What put this idea in your head?" I started to tell him but he kept talking: "Have you really thought about having a hole in your ear?" I was so stressed out from "thinking about it" that I kinda shouted, "YES!" Then I backed off and said as calmly as I could, "Mom has made me think and think and *think* about it." Then he sat and looked at me for a long time, just like Mom (they've lived together *way* too long). I was sure he was going to say no, but instead I got, "I'm not going to give you an answer right now. I want to talk this over with your mom." (Oh great.) *"And . . .* you need to think about it a little more. Do you really want to mutilate your body?" (Hey, Dad, it's one earring, not a plate through my lip!)

I said, "OK." I wasn't too happy about it but what else could I say? He didn't fool me. I knew me thinking more about "mutilating" my body had nothing to do with anything. He just wanted a chance to talk to Mom to see which one of them would be the mean parent who said no.

So today I told him I still really wanted an earring. He looked at me a long, long time . . . again. (I wonder what grown-ups think about when they stare at you like that.) Then he kinda smiled and said, "I really hope you know what you're doing, but if you really think you want someone to jam a needle in your ear, get it all infected so that it swells up like a balloon, infects the side of your face and your ear almost drops off, OK, go for it." He said I could tell Mom what "we" decided so she could make all the arrangements.

SHOCK!! I couldn't believe it!

So Mom took me to a jewelry store this afternoon and told the guy I wanted my ear pierced. Even he looked kinda surprised. That's when I started feeling a little nervous, like everyone knew something I didn't. He made me and Mom sign a release (what . . . in case I die or something?) and had me sit in a barber's chair. This was it. It was really going to happen! The jeweler rubbed my ear with alcohol and my hands started to shake. He got a purple marking pen and said, "Now where did you want the earring?" and I started sweatin'. I looked at Mom and all she did was shrug her shoulders, so the guy put a dot on my left ear and asked if that was OK. I said, "Yeah, sure," even though I didn't see where he put the mark. He could have put it on my nose for all I knew. I was hoping Mom didn't see how bad my hands were shaking or how white my face was.

Then he got this huge nail-gun thing out of a drawer and I started to feel a little sick. He put an earring in it and put it up to my ear. He said he was going to count to three and shoot. *Shoot?!* What do you mean . . . shoot? It was just about then I got really scared. The earring in the puncher thing was as big as a nail and he was gonna "shoot" it through my ear . . . no painkiller, no ice cube, no laughing gas like the dentist . . . *nothing!* I was thinking maybe I had just made a real bad decision when he started to count to three and shot me . . . on *"two"*!

Mom said I jumped but it really didn't hurt that much. My ear started to get warm and I felt a little dizzy, and when I got off the chair my legs felt all limp and rubbery, but it really didn't hurt that much. I have to leave this earring in for six weeks and keep it real clean. Mom keeps asking if this is what I want. "You know, dear, if you take the earring out now, it will probably heal completely and won't even show." (She's almost begging.) I have to talk to her like she's a little kid or something. "Relax, Mom. I'm sure I want this. It will be OK."

. . .

I still can't believe they let me get my ear pierced. This is so cool! Except it kind of hurts to lie on my left side. Can't tell Mom. We all know what she'd say. That's OK. I'll just lie on my right side—for six weeks.

13

Secrets

Thursday, July 19

Aaron called and told me something I can't tell anyone. He spent the night at Stach's last night and while Stach's mom was gone to work they had some beer and got drunk. Now Aaron feels real sick. He threw up all night and had to go home. And he has a bad headache and says his stomach still hurts. He says he feels real dumb, but that Stach called him a baby and said it wouldn't hurt to try a little. Aaron said it didn't taste very good, but he drank it anyway. He just held his nose.

His mom thinks he has the flu. I think he has brain damage.

14

It's All My Fault

Tuesday, July 24

Thunder got hit by a car! He's at the vet. Dad says it's real bad. The vet had to put pins and rods and stuff in Thunder's hip and leg. It sounds terrible. They don't really know if he'll get better. He may limp for the rest of his life or maybe not walk at all. He could even die! No one knows it, but it's all my fault.

Thunder has a big dog run in the side yard and it's right next to the gate. We have a rule that the gate always stays locked because one time Thunder jumped up on it, opened it, and got out. It was a mess. He chased someone's cat up a tree, the neighbors complained, and Dad said he could have been picked up by the dog catcher and taken to the pound or he could have been hit by a car. Anyway, I was playing war games with Aaron and Stach and was running through the backyard and through Thunder's dog run and out the gate. I didn't even think about locking it. Later I went to Aaron's house to play video games. While I was gone, Thunder got the gate open and started running around the neighborhood (looking for me I guess). He must have been real determined to find me because he went clear out onto the main road outside our neighborhood and that's when he got hit.

For a couple of days all Wyatt could do was cry and Dad kept stomping around the house—mad at the cars that go too fast up and down the road. He said he was ready to shoot out tires. And the whole time I'm thinking, "This is all *my* fault." But what was even worse is they thought it was Chelsea who left the gate unlocked because she's done it about a couple hundred times. So even though she kept saying she didn't do it, everyone was kind of mean to her because they thought she did. Mom kept saying things like, "Now, Chelsea, you need to be real honest with me," and Chelsea would yell, "I am!" Wyatt even called her a "big, fat liar" and made her cry.

At night I lay in bed thinking and thinking, "What if Thunder dies? It will be all my fault!" I didn't know what to do. Finally I got brave enough to ask Mom if we could have a talk. I just couldn't stand it anymore. All I could do was sit in my room and worry and feel so bad and my stomach hurt all the time and it wasn't getting any better. That's when I told her about how it was me that left the gate unlocked. I felt so bad when I told her, I almost cried. I felt tears come into my eyes and my stomach hurt even worse. I told her I didn't *mean* to hurt Thunder and that it was just an accident. She got so mad! "Accident? Accident?! How, in your wildest dreams, can you think this was *just* an accident? I can't believe you could be so irresponsible. You never think about anyone but yourself!" When I said, "I just forgot," she got madder and said, "It's not only that you forgot to lock the gate, that's bad enough. But you didn't say a word! You just let everyone blame poor Chelsea." Then she said something that really made me feel like scum, "I don't understand how you could watch Thunder *and* Chelsea suffer" (and she really emphasized "suffer") "and not say anything. *What kind of a boy are you?*" Then she sent me to my room saying, "I'm just too mad to talk to you right now."

Everything had just gone from bad to worse! Then a most amazing thing happened. Mom came into my room and *apologized* for losing her temper! I'm the one who did a really stupid thing and *she* apologized for losing her temper and for being cruel. She hugged me and started talking like she does when she wants me to a learn a lesson. I don't remember everything she said, but she said something about "consequences" and "taking responsibility for my actions." I thought she meant I was going to be punished.

"I want you to understand something, Dean. No one planned Thunder getting hurt, it was the consequence of you forgetting to lock the gate." She kind of lost me there for a while . . . "natural consequences of my actions" and all, but then she said something I *did* understand. "I know how much you love Thunder and you feel pretty lousy now. I hate to tell you this, but you're going to feel lousy for quite a while. I think that's punishment enough."

I thought about that and Mom's right. And it's not just because I don't want her to punish me. Thunder almost died just because I forgot to lock the gate. I wish I could go back and make it all different. Every night since it happened I've lain in bed and wished I could wake up and it would all be a bad dream.

Right before she left, she hugged me again and told me she was glad I told her. "I love you, Dean, just as much as you love Thunder. I'm glad you told me the truth, even if it did take you a while. I respect you for that. But I hope you realize that telling the truth doesn't make everything all right. Thunder is still in serious condition, Chelsea won't come out of her room, Wyatt keeps crying, and your dad is mad at the whole world. In the future, think before you act." (I really felt like crying then.) Just as she was leaving the room, she said, "You might want to apologize to Chelsea and the rest of the family." (I thought she said she wasn't going to punish me.)

So that night during dinner, I told everyone the whole story. I could tell Mom had already told Dad, but you should've seen Wyatt and Chelsea. I think if they had had a rope, they would have hung me! But the worst part was apologizing to Chelsea. I told her I was sorry I let everyone be mad at her. She turned red and started crying and yelled, "I hate you. And I don't want to look at you ever again!" And she ran to her bedroom. Mom went after her. And me, Dad, and Wyatt just sat there at the dinner table. No one said anything. I wasn't very hungry, so I just asked to be excused and went to my room.

A little while later Mom and Chelsea came in to see me. Mom said Chelsea had something she wanted to say. Chelsea didn't look like she wanted to say anything to me ever again. But she said, "I'm sorry I said 'I hate you,' but I don't like you very much right now . . ." Mom nudged her a little. "And I forgive you." Then she ran out crying.

I don't think she's forgiven me. In fact, I don't think she meant a word she said (except where she said she didn't like me). She was just saying what Mom told her to say.

· · ·

Now that everyone knows, I thought I'd feel better. But I don't. I wish so hard this had never happened. I feel miserable.

· · ·

Sunday, August 5

Thunder comes home tomorrow. He's doing OK and is healing a lot better than the vet thought he would. He has a cast on his leg. We have to make sure he takes it easy. I am so happy! I don't know what I would have done if he had died. Now if Chelsea would just lighten up. She really hates me this time.

15

Ticks and Campers' Stew

Life is a lot simpler when it's just "us men." Dad, Wyatt, and I got to go on a camping trip, only the three of us. Dad said he thought maybe we needed to get out of the house for a while. Chelsea still seems pretty mad about what I did, so Dad thought she could use a break from us (from me) and maybe being alone with Mom would help. Mom can usually talk anyone into just about anything. Look at me. She's got me writing in a journal.

Dad said I could invite Aaron, but I guess Aaron had something planned for the weekend with Stach and said he couldn't come. I didn't think camping with just Wyatt and

Dad would be all that great, but it was really fun. We went up in the mountains about fifty miles. There're huge trees and it's lots cooler up there. We pitched the tent and made a campfire. When we got hungry, we cooked campers' stew. It's really neat how you can wrap hamburger, carrots, and potatoes in a foil package and put it in the coals and it will cook perfect. Well, almost perfect. Wyatt's carrots were a little black on the edges, and Dad's whole package got a little burned because it accidentally fell into the middle of the fire. I guess I shouldn't have tried to turn it over with a stick, but I was just trying to make sure it got done on both sides. Anyway, everything tasted pretty good and Dad just cut the burned parts off his food. Then he heated some water and we had hot chocolate. We roasted marshmallows and made s'mores (what would a camping trip be without s'mores?). They were good, but we ate too many. Wyatt's stomach hurt and I was so full I thought I would bust. It was pretty dark when we finally cleaned up camp (you know, so we didn't attract bears or cougars or forest rangers). Then Dad told us ghost stories and we went to bed. Wyatt couldn't sleep at first because he was scared, so Dad let him snuggle by him and told him a little-kid story, the one he always makes up about "The Runaway Penny." This time Dad made the penny run away with a little boy on a camping trip. Before it was over, Wyatt was asleep.

. . .

I really like to go camping. It's neat to lie in the tent with only my nose sticking out of the sleeping bag and listen to the fire crackle and all the crickets and Dad snoring. It makes me feel kind of peaceful and quiet inside. (Kind of weird, huh?)

. . .

The next morning we went for a long hike and Dad told us about the trees and flowers and animals and bugs. We saw some deer tracks and wild strawberries and I think I saw some cougar tracks. When we got back to camp, Dad gave us pocketknives and let us carve and whittle. Dad got a long stick and cut Wyatt's initials in it so it could be Wyatt's personal walking stick. I tried to make a cougar, but when it was done it looked more like a dog, so I decided it was Thunder. Wyatt had a great time hacking at his piece of wood, making nothing but a mess. It doesn't take much to keep little kids happy.

That night we had regular hamburgers and beans. Dad heated the beans right in the can over the fire. It was so cool until he tried to pick it up with the tongs and the whole can fell into the fire. Sure made the fire smell funny for a while. It was lucky Mom sent two cans of beans. I guess she knows camping trips are full of accidents. When it got dark, we didn't have to worry about Wyatt. He was asleep almost before Dad could zip up his sleeping bag.

Dad and I stayed up late and he told me about when he

was a kid and would catch fireflies and put them in a jar and pretend it was a lantern. And about his paper route and all the crazy people he met, like the lady who had two hundred cats. Dad said you could smell her house three blocks away and he would almost turn blue (from trying to hold his breath) when he went to collect for the paper. He said he almost died the time she invited him in for some cookies; he had to take three showers when he got home and still couldn't get rid of the smell, and his mom made him eat dinner out in the garage. I don't know if that part was true. I can't believe Grandma Matthews would make any kid eat out in the garage. She's just way too cool.

He started telling me about a camping trip he went on, just him and his big brother, my uncle Dean, but Dad started coughing and rubbing his eyes. I guess the smoke from the fire got in his face. When I asked him what happened on the camping trip, he said, "Nothing, never mind. It's time to get some shut-eye."

Right before we fell asleep I told Dad I wished we could do stuff like camping all the time. Dad said, "Sure, we'll do more 'stuff.' And next time, maybe we should bring the ladies." He meant Mom and Chelsea. I guess that's all right, but it was really cool with just us men.

. . .

When we got back from camping, the first thing Mom said was, "You all stink!" (Yeah, like *real* men.) "Hit the showers." When Mom was drying Wyatt's hair, she found a tick on the back of his neck. So Wyatt started panting like he does right before he's going to cry, but Mom told him not to worry. (Right! There's a gigantic bloodsucker latched onto your neck, but don't worry, Wyatt. He won't drink too much.) Señora Ana got some alcohol and smeared it all over the tick. She said it would make it pull its head out. We watched and the tick started to move but it didn't pull all the way out. So Mom said, "I think we better get the tweezers," and Wyatt started whimpering, "No, no, no, no." Dad got the big tweezers, Mom held Wyatt's hand, and Wyatt started yelling, "OW, OW, OW," before Dad even touched him. And all the time Chelsea was jumping up and down telling Wyatt not to be such a big baby. In the middle of all the confusion, Dad just pulled the whole tick out. It even had a little bit of Wyatt's skin in its jaws (or whatever they have). Chelsea was so grossed out she went screaming into her room.

When it was out, me, Dad, and Wyatt were looking at it. The tick was just sitting there. I asked Dad if we should flush it down the toilet, but he said no. He had to take the tick and Wyatt to the doctor. So Wyatt really started howling and crying! But Dad said they had to go. He said there are some ticks that can make you real sick. But as it turned out, everything was OK. I checked my hair too since Señora Ana says that's where ticks like to "dig in." (I liked her little joke.)

Now Wyatt's going around telling everyone about his

tick. Dad let him keep it in a jar of alcohol and he's showing it to everyone like it was a prize or something. And he's
telling everyone that he almost died from the tick, and that
they had to dig it out with a knife because it had a real long
stinger, but he didn't cry or scream or anything. Little kids
are so weird.

. . .

*Wyatt having a tick turned out pretty darn good. With all
the excitement (and grossing out) I think Chelsea forgot
about being mad at me. She's acting pretty normal . . . at
least for Chelsea. I think everything's going to be all OK.
I may say mean things about her, but it was really the pits
when she hated me. I'm glad Chelsea doesn't hate me anymore.*

16

All Grown Up?

Wednesday, August 29

I hope no one ever finds out. Especially Mom and Dad. I'd probably be grounded for life!

I got to spend the night at Aaron's house last night. His parents went to a movie and we stayed home. We had a good time, kind of, I guess. We played video games and went swimming in his pool. Then Aaron asked did I want to try some beer. First I told him no, but he said it was OK to try just a little and that it wasn't such a bad thing as long as you didn't drink too much. So I said OK.

It tasted terrible! Aaron said to just hold my nose and drink a whole lot at once. It still tasted bad. Then he said he could beat me drinking the rest of the bottle, so we raced. Then he got out two more bottles even though I didn't want any more. He said only babies are afraid to try new things, so I went ahead and drank half the bottle while he guzzled his. About that time my stomach started feeling crummy, and I couldn't close my eyes without getting dizzy. I told him I didn't want any more, so he drank the rest of mine. Then he got another one and started acting real stupid. He was jumping on the couch and the chairs and playing the music real loud and spraying me with beer. All of a sudden he went racing out of the room. I went to see what was going on, and there he was, throwing his guts up in the toilet. I left to give him some privacy, but when he didn't come out I went to see if he was OK. And there he was, fast asleep on the bathroom floor. I tried to get him up, but he wasn't budging. I knew his mom and dad would be home soon so I got a cold rag and put it on his face so he would wake up. I walked him into the family room and he plopped down on the couch and fell asleep again. I didn't sleep very well all night, but Aaron did. He was still asleep when I left this morning.

When I got home, I hurried into the bathroom without saying hi or anything. I just knew if Mom saw me she would be able to tell I'd been drinking. I got in the shower just in case there was still some smell left on me. All of a sudden someone was pounding on the door. I almost fell out of the tub. It was Mom! "Just checking. I didn't know you were home. Did you have a good time?" (Oh yeah, Mom, just a *super great time.) Then she said, "I'm glad you came home early. We have lots to do around the house today. I'm just going to grab your clothes. I'm getting ready to do some wash." My clothes! I'd forgotten about them. I should've kept them on while I took the shower. With all the beer Aaron sprayed on me while he was going crazy they had to smell like a bar. I didn't know what to do. I could hear the door open, then close. I held my breath figuring it was only a matter of seconds before she came tearing through the door, fire in her eyes, bellowing like a dragon. But she never came back, and she never said anything.*

I ended up staying in the shower for about twenty minutes trying to get my heart to slow down. Now I know why doctors are always telling you drinking is bad for your health. It almost gave me a heart attack!

Wow! I've written three full pages! I've never written that much at one time. Amazing what staring death in the face can do to a guy.

17

School Has Started Again

Tuesday, September 4

What a way to ruin a perfectly good summer—school. And as usual, the first day was A TOTAL DISASTER! Summer was way too short.

First I couldn't get my locker to work. Every time I did the combination it wouldn't open until this kid said I was doing it all wrong. I have to pass the second number once before stopping at it the *second* time (duh). Then at lunch a bunch of big ninth graders grabbed me and shoved me in my locker and closed the door. Oh, real funny . . . real mature!

At first I thought they would let me right out, but they ran away when the bell rang. I didn't know what to do. It started to get real cramped and hot, and I got kinda nervous so I started pounding the locker with my head (because it was the only thing I could move) and yelling for someone to let me out. Then I heard this girl say, "Are you all right?" (Oh, sure. I'm just chillin' in here. I think I'll spend the rest of seventh grade *in my locker!*) I asked her to *please* let me out. She said, "Sure thing. What's your combination?" Uh . . . my combination? Oh yeah, my combination. Those three little numbers I haven't memorized yet so I wrote them on my hand that I can't move because of being crammed in this stupid locker and even if I could get my hand up to my face I wouldn't be able to read it because **IT IS PITCH DARK IN HERE!**

She said she would go get help. She was gone an awful long time. Finally I heard footsteps coming up to my locker. They didn't sound like a girl's. I held my breath. Then I heard the combination being turned and the door opened. I almost fell out 'cause my legs had gone to mush. I looked up, and there stood the vice principal, the one you have to go to when you get in trouble and he gives you detention for life. I knew I was dead meat. But he just shook his head and said, "I know it doesn't help much, but you're not the first. Now get to class."

. . .

Why me? Why always me? I know the whole story is going to be all over school tomorrow. You watch. I'll be branded for life as the "little seventh grade kid who got stuffed in his locker." And then everyone will have to try it at least once. It will be the new sport at Fillmore Junior High—"Who can shove little Dean Matthews in his locker the most times," with a special award for anyone who can keep him in there for a whole day. And I'm sure I'll have a whole section of the yearbook so that no one ever forgets. I hate school and I hate being a seventh grader! I hate being a little shrimpy seventh grader!

18

Bill Crocket

Wednesday, September 12

I met a new kid this week. His name is Bill Crocket, just like Davy Crockett, but he says he's not related. Too bad. Aaron says he has an ancestor who was a pirate. His mom does family history stuff and they found out they're related to some famous pirate . . . Bluebeard or someone. That is just too cool. I wonder if my family is related to anyone exciting? (Yeah right, my family.)

Anyway, Bill Crocket is pretty cool. He just moved into our neighborhood (three houses down). He's from Seattle (where it rains all the time). He's in two of my classes (science & math). His locker is right next to mine, and we have

something really important in common . . . he has an ear-
ring in his left ear too.

We were talking about it and I was telling him how I get
teased once in a while about my earring, you know, stupid
ninth graders who ask me when I'm going to start wearing
nail polish and lipstick. He said no one ever teases him
mainly because he's so tall and big (he looks like a high
school football player). He says when he first got his ear
pierced, a couple of guys tried to tease him but he just
looked "down" on them and said, "The last guy who teased
me about my earring was in traction for three months."
That's pretty cool, but I don't think it would work for me.
Dad says I'm more the "tennis player" type (I think he's trying to tell me I'm short and skinny without hurting my feelings). I can just see me using that line on some guy and *ME*
ending up in traction for three months.

   I asked Bill how many guys he's beat up. He really surprised me. He said, "Fighting is stupid. I don't believe in
it. I'd rather talk my way out of trouble and if that doesn't
work, I bluff." I was thinking maybe he was a coward but
he said, "Besides, fighting doesn't prove anything except
that you can use your fists instead of your head." I said,
"Sounds like something my dad would say." He laughed
and admitted that it is the standard lecture at his house. "Besides," he said, "the only time I did get in a fight, I ended

up in a world full of trouble and I wasn't even the one who started it. It's just not worth it."

So I got to thinking, maybe he's right. I'm never gonna be able to come out of a fight proving anything except that I bleed real good. So maybe bluffing would work for me.

. . .

I might just have to hang out with Bill Crocket and see if I can pick up a few pointers. He's pretty cool.

19

Bullies

Thursday, September 20

Aaron is in so much trouble. He has detention for a month. What is going on with him? It doesn't make any sense.

One of the kids in his P.E. class told me all about it. He said Aaron was pushing Sam around. Sam's a Vietnamese kid who moved here last year. We call him Sam because no one can pronounce his real name. He speaks pretty good English and does real good in school. He's little—littler than even me. And he's kind of shy and keeps to himself. I don't know him very well, I hardly even notice him. Anyway, Aaron was pretending to karate kick him, so Mr. Howard yelled and warned him to stop. Then I guess after class, Aaron snuck up behind Sam in the locker room and got him in a headlock and threw him on the floor and kind of hurt him. Then he started calling Sam a baby and a wimp and pretending to talk Vietnamese and making fun of him. Bill's in the same P.E. class and I guess he got pretty mad and said, "Leave the kid alone!" So Aaron turned around and started swearing at Bill and told him to mind his own business. That's when Mr. Howard walked in and told Aaron to get out and go see the vice principal. Then Aaron started swearing at Mr. Howard!

Bill says Aaron acts like he's on something like drugs. I don't think he's dumb enough to do drugs. When we were in the D.A.R.E. program in fourth grade, we had to write a paper on how bad drugs are and why you shouldn't take them, and Aaron's report was so good they hung it up and the D.A.R.E. cop congratulated him and everything.

I don't know what to think. It's kinda weird thinking about how Aaron acted and how Bill acted. When I first met Aaron he was the one sticking up for little kids (me). In fact, now that I think about it, Aaron and Bill said the same thing: "Leave the kid alone" . . . but now Aaron's the bully.

I called Aaron after school to see if he was OK. He said nothing was wrong. He said he had just had a fight with his dad that morning and had been mad at everyone all day. I asked him if he got in big trouble for getting on detention, but he said no. His dad said detention was enough.

Then he said, "Who the he— is Bill?" And he started swearing again and calling Bill some really rude names. He said he couldn't believe I was friends with Bill. I didn't know what to say so I changed the subject.

I kinda felt like a coward for not sticking up for Bill, but I've known Aaron longer and he's my best friend. I asked if he wanted to ride bikes. He told me he and Stach were going downtown. I asked him if I could go and he got kind of funny on the phone and said he would have to ask Stach. He said he would call me back. He never called.

20

Science Projects— Part One

Tuesday, September 25

I hate science projects. I never know what to do. Am I suppose to invent something or discover something? I sometimes wish I was still in elementary school because all you had to do was grow a bunch of plants in the dark or stick some celery in blue water or make a volcano that exploded and everyone would think you were wonderful and smile and say, "What a bright little boy." But then you go to junior high and they expect you to do calculus or invent time travel.

I don't think anyone really cares about the stuff in science projects. You don't see any important scientists coming and getting all excited about blue celery or volcanoes. I wonder if I could fake getting sick for a couple of months?

21

The Dance

Friday, October 5

We had our first seventh grade dance. What a joke!

They had it right after school today. The boys stood on one side of the room and the girls stood on the other side and no one would walk over and ask anyone to dance. There we were, a bunch of cowardly dorks, looking at each other while the music went on and on, and the teachers looked real nervous. It was so exciting, I almost fell asleep. That is, until the very end.

One of the girls finally walked over and asked Bill to dance. We were all laughing and making fun of him. He looked so stupid out there. And then one of the girls came over and asked *me* to dance! It wouldn't have been so bad except she's about a foot taller than me. Oh, we looked real good together . . . the wimp and the amazon. Why do these things always happen to me?

· · ·

I don't know if I'll go to another dance. They're kind of dumb. Señora Ana says someday I'll like them. Yeah right.

22

A Day at the Mall

Saturday, October 6

I've really done it this time! All I did was go to the mall with Aaron and Stach. I told Mom that it was just me and Aaron. I figured she'd say no if she knew Stach would be along. I don't think she likes him very much. Every time I talk about him, she gets kind of a sour look on her face, and if his name comes up when I ask to do something, she usually says no. But we were just going to the mall. What could go wrong? Real stupid question.

Since the weather was so good and the mall isn't far away, we decided to take our bikes. Mom said that would be OK, and then she added, "Be careful. Be smart." I wish I had followed her advice.

We ate lunch in the food court, then went to the computer store to play the new computer games. The manager finally came over and asked if we were with our parents and when Stach said, "What's it to ya?" he asked us to leave. Then we went to the toy and hobby store and looked at all the stuff. Everything was pretty cool and we were having a good time with all the demo toys, until, well, I guess you could say everything that happened after that was *my* fault. All I said was "I sure wish I was rich so I could buy all this stuff." So Stach said, "You don't have to be rich," and he winked and opened his hand. He had some baseball cards. "Just take what you want." Then he told Aaron to go do it. So Aaron went to another aisle and I guess he took something. Then Stach told me I had to steal something. I said, "We're going to get caught!" So he starts to make chicken noises. "You're a chicken. A little baby chicken." So I hurried and grabbed a ball (just a little one). Then we saw one of the guys who worked at the store. It was time to get outta there. We were just outside the store when the guy came running after us, grabbed me and Aaron by the arm and said, "Shoplifting is a crime." I thought I was gonna die! And where was Stach? He was halfway down the mall! He never even looked back.

The guy took us to his office and told us to empty our pockets. I just had the ball but Aaron had four packs of baseball cards. The store guy started yelling at us and asked who the other kid was. Aaron said, "I don't know." I didn't know what to say so I just sat there acting dumb (which I'm real good at), hoping I could just disappear or fall through the floor. But then it got worse . . . he called our parents!

When Mom and Dad got there, the manager said he would forget the whole thing if we would pay for the toys (such a big deal over a fifty-nine-cent ball). Then he told Mom that Aaron had taken something too and so had the other kid. Mom said, "What *other* kid?" I told her it was Stach. Boy did she look mad, but she just told the man Stach's name and address. He thanked her but said, "There's not much we can do once they leave the premises. Most of these kids get rid of the things they take pretty fast." Then he said I could go home with my parents. Aaron's parents still hadn't come so he had to stay.

I thought for sure Mom and Dad (well, at least Mom) would start yelling the minute we left the store, but they didn't say a thing. I could tell Dad was pretty mad though, by the way he threw (and I mean *threw*) my bike into the back of the truck. They didn't say a thing all the way home and then they just told me to go to my room. That was as bad as being yelled at—sitting there, sweatin' it out, wondering what they were going to do to me.

I could kinda hear them talking through their door. I couldn't hear everything they were saying, but I thought I heard something about "criminal behavior" and "grounded for life." I snuck out of my room and I was close to their door to try to hear more when Chelsea came up behind me and asked me what I was doing. She about scared me to death, so I whispered, "Mind your own business and get out of here or I'll kick your . . . !" She stuck her tongue out at me and started singing, "I'm gonna tell! I'm gonna tell on *you!*" Then I really got mad and sorta shoved her. Just then Dad opened the door. Man, when I decide to get in trouble, I go *all* the way! Dad told Chelsea to go play. Then he turned to me and looked real mad. "Don't you think you're in enough trouble? Since you're eavesdropping, you might as well join us."

He told me to sit on the bed (so they could look down on me) and said it was time for the complete truth. I asked Mom if this was an amnesty talk but Dad said, "Not on your life!" Then it started—the inquisition.

"Have you ever stolen anything before?"

"No."

"Is there any reason you decided now was the time to start your criminal career?"

"Well, Stach and Aaron did it and called me chicken."

"Sounds like a pretty sad excuse." (Yeah, sounded pretty lame even to me.)

Then they wanted to know more about Stach. I told them about his mom and dad being divorced and that he's usually pretty cool. Then Dad yelled, "Hey, guy, stealing isn't cool! Prison isn't cool! And picking friends like Stach isn't cool!" He was starting to get pretty hot when Mom gave him a look like, "Chill out, dear." Then Mom asked me if I thought it was such a good idea to hang around with Stach if he did stuff like stealing. I tried to explain to her that Aaron was my best friend and since Aaron hung around with Stach, then I wanted to hang around with Stach. So Mom said, "Oh, and if your best friend jumps off a cliff, would you do it too?" What a stupid question. Why does she do that? I never know what to say. I get in trouble if I try to answer, but they get mad if I just sit there trying to look pathetic. But before I could even try to answer she said, "Getting in this kind of trouble is definitely not cool and it's going to cost you big time!"

I couldn't believe it! It was so unfair. The ball only cost fifty-nine cents and I've never done anything like this before. And I didn't even really want to. Stach told us to do it. It was all Stach's fault.

Then Dad started yelling again (I couldn't believe he was yelling, he never yells), "You should feel pretty lucky things aren't worse." (Oh yeah, I feel *real* lucky.) "You know, the store could have called the police, and if the police get involved, you have a record."

· · ·

I'm still shaking. That's the scaredest I've ever been. And I'm MAD! Mad at Mom and Dad—mad at Chelsea—

mad at me—but especially mad at Stach. That stupid Stach,
getting us into trouble like that and then taking off.

．　．　．

Later, when I was allowed out of my cell, I called Aaron. He got grounded for two weeks. His dad yelled a lot and his mom cried. Then they asked him if he had learned his lesson and he said yes. *That was it!* That's all the grief he had to put up with. But he said he was pretty scared too. He said his parents didn't want him to hang around Stach anymore. "And I kinda think they're right," he said. "We always seem to get into trouble for something. Maybe you and me should just hang out together from now on." (Yeah, like the old days.)

Maybe I'll ask Mom if he can spend the night next weekend. Oh right, fat chance. I'm stuck in "Matthews Prison" for a couple of centuries. But maybe if I look real sorry and tell her Aaron and I want to spend more time together like we used to before Stach came along she'll let him. She's always liked Aaron a lot. He brought her flowers once for her birthday (I think they were really from Mrs. Timmons but Mom made such a big deal about it, he took all the credit). Anyway, maybe she'll talk to Aaron's mom so he can stay over even though he's grounded.

Actually, I think Aaron's parents just want him grounded from Stach.

23

Changes

Saturday, October 13

Things sure are different than they used to be. It can get complicated when you start to grow up.

Even after all the trouble, Aaron's mom said he could spend the night as long as he was home by nine o'clock in the morning *and* we had to stay close to home and always be with my parents. It was kinda like in the prison movies where they let you out in the yard for some exercise, but someone is always watching you. Still, we had a pretty good time. Mom took us to Telly's Pizza Place and we played video games and rode the gyrosphere. We tried to talk Mom into trying it, but Dad must have told her about it and she laughed and said, "Do I have 'stupid' written somewhere on my forehead? Forget it!" On the way home we rented a couple of karate movies and had popcorn and even though we went to bed early, Mom let us talk until late. Aaron told me about other times he's been with Stach and they stole things. One time Stach cut a guy's tires, and they sprayed graffiti on some people's fences. He told me about a couple of times he went over to Stach's house and drank beer *and* whiskey. He said Stach made him do all that stuff.

. . .

I can't believe everything he's done! Where have I been?

After he left, it felt so weird. We used to have so many fun and crazy times. We used to laugh so hard we could hardly breathe. I would always wish he could stay over forever. But this time I was almost glad when he left. Not really glad, but it's like I don't know him anymore. He's not the same as he used to be and it's not as easy to talk to him. We don't laugh about the same things anymore. We don't seem to be the same kind of friends. I mean, I still really like him, he's still my best friend, I think. But something's different.

Sometimes I wish things wouldn't change.

24

Einstein and Cleopatra

Saturday, October 20

My life is so boring, nothing exciting ever happens. I'm working on my science project and doing other school-work, and doing housework for Mom and having to play with my brother and sister because family is the most im-portant thing and not getting to do anything fun. What a boring, boring life. I'm so bored . . . bored . . . bored . . . bored!

Funny how if you write a word enough times it starts to look like it's spelled wrong. Like the other day. I was writing a paper in school about *"Why school is important to our lives,"* and after about the fiftieth time I spelled "school" it didn't look right anymore. So I tried spelling it a couple of different ways just to be sure. When I got my paper back I got a C+. Miss Eames told me I didn't need to be such a "smart aleck" messing up the word "school" like I did. (I was just making sure it was spelled right somewhere on my paper.)

But back to my science project. I decided to do a project with mice to see which learns better, boys or girls. I know it's a lame idea but it was a good way to get a couple of pets. And besides, I already know the answer. The boy mouse is smarter, just like boy humans. I've named him Einstein. Chelsea said to name the girl mouse Giggles. Yeah right! No science project of mine is going to be named "Giggles," so I named her Cleopatra.

I've designed a maze with tunnels and turns and stuff—toilet paper rolls make great mice tunnels. Mom got a little irritated when she found all the toilet paper on the bathroom floor, but what could I do? We didn't have any *empty* toilet paper rolls. Anyway, every day I let the mice run through the maze. The first time they did it, Einstein just sat there like a dumb idiot. He took fifteen minutes to get through the maze. Cleopatra was so hyper that even though she made a lot of wrong turns, she still made it through the maze in about a minute and a half. I started to wonder if the guy at the pet store had told me wrong—that the one he said was a girl was really a boy and vice versa. But the more I run them through the maze, the better Einstein gets. He's improved his time and Cleopatra still just kind of bounces off the walls until she finds her way out. Einstein now takes a little less than a minute to go through the maze and Cleopatra takes anywhere from one to five minutes to get through. So I guess I've discovered what everyone knows: Boys are definitely smarter than girls.

Now comes the part I really, *really* hate. I have to write all this stuff up in a report and make a presentation board (like I'm not already doing enough writing).

. . .

I really hate science projects. But I guess that's OK. Mom really hates the rodents.

25

A Benevolent
Dictatorship

Friday, October 26

*There should be a law that says parents have to be fair.
Of course, Mom has her own definition of fair, so it probably wouldn't help.*

I decided I want a second earring, but when I told Mom,
she just laughed and said, "When pigs fly." (Oh, real intelligent thing to say, Mom.) I told her I was serious and she
just kept laughing and said she was serious too. That's when
I made the fatal mistake—I yelled, **"Stop laughing! You
let me have the first earring! You're not being fair!"** She
stopped laughing and got sarcastic. "Fair? My dear young

man, you are in a dream world if you think 'fair' has anything to do with life in this household."

I tried to explain to her (in a calm and mature voice), "I'm not a little kid. I should be able to make *all* my own decisions." The minute I said it, I knew I was in trouble. She started to get mad and said I had plenty of freedom. Well, I was mad too so I kind of sneered at her and said, "Yeah right." (Not the most intelligent thing I could have said, but I never can think of anything good to say until a day or two later.) Then she yelled, *"You'll have a lot less freedom if you don't change your attitude."* For a minute I thought she was going to hit me. Instead, she told me to go to my room. Just like some sort of baby or something. I'm too old for this.

A little later she came in and said she was sorry she lost her temper. So I looked real sincere and said, "That's OK Mom. I understand. Now can we talk about this calmly and rationally?" (I was trying to sound real mature.) She took a deep breath and said, "I might be sorry for losing my temper, but it doesn't change anything." And then I got "the lecture" about how I have a lot of freedom, as much as I can handle, and that it doesn't seem I appreciate the freedom I have and that with freedom comes responsibility and blah . . . blah . . . blah. When I tried to argue some more with her, she said, "You are operating under the false notion that you have a vote on all issues. I'm sorry to inform you that this household is *not* a democracy. I may let you voice an opinion and occasionally allow you some freedom, but as supreme dictator, I get to wreck and rule your life until you're eighteen. Learn to accept that, my dear. You'll be a happier person." Then she walked out giggling at herself.

I wanted to scream and hit something, hard.

. . .

She can act so . . . so . . . stupid sometimes. And she thought she was so funny. Yeah right. I wonder what she'd do if I just showed up one day with a second earring . . . and a tattoo across my chest . . . riding a Harley-Davidson motorcycle . . . with a cigarette hanging out of my mouth!! I can't wait until I'm eighteen.

26

Dead Men and Missing Bikes

Thursday, November 1

Mom's right. Life isn't fair. It's either ruined by little sisters or wrecked by jerks you don't even know.

We had a Halloween carnival at school last night. Our science class did a spook alley to raise money for a field trip. I was supposed to be a dead guy who sat up out of a coffin and groaned every time someone walked by, and I would grab at them. I was all bloody and gross with one eye hanging out. It was great scaring everyone, especially the girls.

Then Mom brought Wyatt and Chelsea. Chelsea screamed so loud, I thought she was going to wet her pants and faint. It was great until all of a sudden she stopped right in the middle of the spook alley and yelled, "Oh, Dean, I know it's you!" Then she stood there and told everyone coming through, "Don't be scared, it's just my brother Dean." She kept pointing to where I was and telling everyone I was going to jump out and try to scare them. She was spoiling everything and all Mom would do was laugh. I yelled at her to get Chelsea out of there, but she just kept laughing and pointing down at Wyatt.

And there was Wyatt. I had definitely scared him, so bad in fact that he had his arms wrapped around Mom's legs and wouldn't let go. His eyes were shut so tight his face was scrunched and he was yelling, "I want out!" Mom tried to pull his arms away from around her legs, but that just made him yell louder and hold tighter. The more she tried to get him to let loose, the louder he yelled, and Mom kept laughing harder and harder, and Chelsea was having such a good time playing "tour guide" to my corner, "Come and see how scary my brother Dean looks. He's right over here. Hi, Dean, you can scare them now." I could have killed them all.

Finally Mom was able to get Wyatt to let loose of her legs long enough to pick him up. He immediately wrapped his fat little arms around her head and his chubby legs around her waist in a death grip. She kinda looked like a mummy. (Get it? My mommy looked like a "mummy." It's a joke. I guess you would've had to be there.)

Anyway, Mom was still laughing when they left and Chelsea kept turning around yelling, "Good-bye, Dean. Be a good dead guy." (Sometimes I can't believe I'm related to these people.)

When I got home Chelsea said she was sorry and Mom said she was sorry too. And then Wyatt said he was sorry, but I could tell he didn't know what the heck he was sorry for and that Mom had just told him to say it. Then Mom (peacemaker and benevolent dictator) said, "You have to admit, Dean, it *was* kind of funny. At least everyone going through the spook alley thought it was. I bet it was the first spook alley where everyone came out laughing." And all three of them started giggling again. I was not amused.

Then to top the evening off, my bike got stolen. It must have happened while we were at the carnival. I guess I forgot to put it inside our fence and left it out all night. When I went to get it this morning, it was gone. I don't see how anybody could've seen it. It's dark on the side of the house and someone just driving by wouldn't see it. Why would anyone want to take my bike? It's not a top-of-the-line mountain bike or an expensive racing bike or even one of those trick bikes. Then Mom started lecturing me about the consequences of irresponsible behavior and that she was really sorry (yeah right), but . . . (and here's where it gets worse) . . . since it was mostly my fault, she won't pay for a new one.

. . .

*Why me? Why always me? Life stinks. And so does who-
ever took my bike!*

Thursday, November 1, 8:30 P.M.!

*Dad to the rescue! He just came to talk to me and said
if I have enough or can save enough for half the bike, he'll
pay for the other half. I asked him if I could take it out of
my savings. He said that's what savings are for, then he got
a funny look on his face. "How much you got, sport?
$1.95?" I loved the way he looked when I told him I had
$125.00!*

*I'd never want to admit it to her, but I'm glad Mom
started making me save half my allowance and birthday
money. Some of Mom's rules actually work. Wonders never
cease.*

27

Science Projects—
Part Two

Saturday, November 10

It's all the teachers' fault! If they wouldn't make us do stupid things like science projects, none of this would have happened.

I went to get the mice so they could run through the maze. Cleopatra was running around the cage real crazylike and burrowing into the sawdust and she had pulled a piece of paper through the cage and had torn it all up. I couldn't figure out what her problem was (but then I can't figure out what *any* girl's problem is). At first I thought she was just anxious to run through the maze. I reached in to get her and she bit me! When I finally put her in the maze, she did a terrible job. She just kept running around in circles and putting her front paws up on the walls of the maze like she was trying to look over it.

The next morning, when I went to feed them, there were babies! I didn't know what to do. I couldn't tell Mom. She didn't like the mice to begin with. And now there were *seven* of them!

But it gets worse (it always gets worse). After school when I went to check on the babies, Einstein had killed them all! It kinda looked like he ate them or chewed on them. It was so gross. I knew I couldn't hide *this* from Mom, so I took my best "so sorry" face to her and told her what happened. She looked kinda surprised and said, "Cleopatra had babies? When did all this happen? Is there a reason I wasn't informed?"

It was a good thing the Science Fair was only two days away. I don't think I could have handled any more stress. I didn't win first place, but I did get third in my category: "Science Projects Using Animals" (never again). I had my presentation board, notebook, the maze, and mice all at school. Einstein and Cleopatra were acting like nothing ever happened (you know, with the babies and all). I put them through the maze for the judges. It didn't exactly work like it did at home. I sent them through ten times and Einstein won most of the time, but two of the times Cleopatra beat the socks off him. (Maybe she was a little mad about the babies.) Anyway, the judges said my record keeping was good, the maze was excellent, and "given all the parameters involved in the proper setup, testing, and follow-through required for a science fair project at this level, Dean Matthews has done an outstanding and thorough job."

．　．　．

Adults sure can take up a lot of words just to say, "Way to go, dude." At least it's over with . . . until next year. I hate science projects.

28

Questions

Saturday, November 17

There was a little excitement in the neighborhood last night. And I saw the whole thing on the TV news.

The cops were patrolling our neighborhood and saw a bunch of kids sneaking around. One of them was pushing a little bike and I guess it looked strange so the cops followed them. They caught a bunch of them in an old shack out in the desert, kinda behind Aaron's house. When they searched the shack, there were a whole bunch of bikes, skateboards, CD players, and even a couple of TVs. But that's not all. Guess who was there? Stach and Aaron.

I still can't believe it. They took all the kids down to the police station and called all their parents. Mom said some of the kids might end up going to jail. Later, Aaron called and said he hadn't stolen anything and didn't know until that night that anybody was stealing anything. He said he was just playing around with Stach the night they got caught.

I'm beginning to be a little suspicious. Even though my bike wasn't in the shack, I wonder if they were the guys who took it. I asked Aaron but he said, "No way!" He said if he found out Stach was the one who stole my bike, he wouldn't be Stach's friend anymore (yeah, I've heard that before). Besides, he said Stach really likes me and wouldn't ever do that to a friend. I guess I said something about Stach not being so cool because Aaron tried to explain him to me. "Stach isn't so bad. He acts the way he does because he feels bad about not having his dad around and sometimes gets real mad at everyone and everything. So he does things because he thinks no one really cares anyway."

.   .   .

I don't know. I guess it would be hard not having a dad around. But I don't know if I would start stealing if I didn't have a dad. I don't know what to believe. Things sure seem to be getting all messed up with Aaron and stealing and Stach and . . . everything. I wish it was last summer.

P.S. As it turned out, Stach didn't have to go to jail or anything. He's back in school. He said they never do anything to kids so he never worries. And he said he didn't take my bike. But he said if I wanted a new one he could get one for me. Yeah right.

29

The Chapter That Almost Wasn't . . .

Saturday, November 24

I wonder if you get life imprisonment for blowing up a school? I came so close to getting in major-league trouble, or blowing myself to smithereens. And I'm not so sure which would've been worse.

We've been talking about explosives in science class and we had to do team reports on a type of explosive. Bill and me and another kid named Jonathan were partners and we decided to do a report on gunpowder. Jonathan got the bright idea that we should demonstrate how to use gunpowder by showing how to build a backyard rocket. He said he and his dad did it once so he knew all about it and it was easy. That should've been our first clue we were headed for disaster. Jonathan is the kid who can never get his locker open, always falls over someone's chair (or his own feet), and blows peas and milk out of his nose when he chokes on his lunch, which is at least twice a week. This kid doesn't have a clue.

But when he talked about the backyard rocket, he made it sound almost intelligent. So yesterday during lunch, we asked Mr. Stevens if we could use the lab to finish our assignment. He said, "Sure." Jonathan brought everything we needed. So far so good. We stuffed the charcoal, sulfur, and saltpeter into an aluminum cigar tube. When I asked Jonathan if he was sure of all the proportions and measurements, he looked kind of confused but said, "I know what I'm doing. What do you think I am? Some kind of dummy?" (That should've been our second clue.)

Jonathan put a fuse on the end of the rocket and it was done. I have to admit, it looked pretty good. I thought for sure this would get us an A. Then Bill said, "Why don't we shoot it off at the end of our report? We could take the whole class out on the old baseball field and shoot it. Everyone will love it!" I said, "What! Are you nuts? We don't even know if it's going to work and if it doesn't work, we will all look so stupid and ruin our grade and besides . . ."

Bill and Jonathan weren't even listening. They were going on and on about how they thought it would be the best way to end our report, and Mr. Stevens would think we were brilliant, and the whole school would talk about us— we would be legends. Then Jonathan said, "But Dean's right. We better test the rocket before to make sure it will work." Things were getting way out of control so I said, "How are we going to *test* it? Shoot it through the ceiling? If we shoot it on school grounds without permission or a teacher around, we'll get caught and suspended or expelled. Let's just forget it."

About this time I could tell Bill was getting pretty irritated at me. So Jonathan (the peacemaker and local idiot) said, "We could build a little ramp and shoot it out the window. It only faces the old baseball field and no one's out there. That way no one will know where it came from and no one will know who did it. Probably no one will even see it. Then if it works, we could repack another one for class and do the same thing." He was getting so excited he was jumping up and down just like a little kid. And that's when it hit me. What was I worried about? With Jonathan as the brains of the outfit, the rocket wasn't going to work, so the test would be a failure and that would be the end of this whole ridiculous matter. So I smiled and said, "Sure. Great. Sounds like a good idea. Let's go for it."

We built the ramp out of our books. Bill opened the window and I made sure the rocket was headed straight out. I even took a yardstick and laid it alongside the rocket to see if it was in a direct line to the window. We all looked so sci-entific and professional, almost like we knew what we were doing. I even started to think our little experiment might work. *Yeah right!*

Bill lit the fuse and we moved back. As we were moving back, Jonathan bumped the desk the rocket was on (big sur-prise) and our ramp shifted. We all looked at each other. I jumped for the rocket but it fired before I could get to it and it didn't exactly fly *out* the window. It did, however, hit the windowsill, bounced off, flew straight toward the ceil-ing, bounced off, headed for us (we ducked), hit the desk and went straight toward the blackboard, bouncing a cou-ple of times off the floor. Then to make the whole mess a complete success, Mr. Stevens walked in just as the rocket whizzed by him (barely missing his nose), bounced off the blackboard, fell into the garbage can and sizzled.

No one said anything. He looked at us. . . . We looked at him. Then he walked over to the garbage can. The rocket was still sizzling. Then as if things weren't bad enough, the rocket kind of blew up in the garbage can. I guess the pro-portions weren't quite right (big duh). It wasn't a very big explosion, but enough to catch the papers in the garbage can on fire. We all just kinda stood there and watched until the fire went out. I could feel my face getting hot and it wasn't from the fire in the garbage can. I wished I could wake up and make this whole nightmare go away. What were we going to tell Mr. Stevens? What was I going to tell Mom and Dad? Better yet, how could we pin this whole mess on Jonathan?

Then a thought occurred to me. Maybe Mom would just laugh and say, "Oh, he's just curious. He looked so cute standing there in the middle of the burned-out lab. Who knows, maybe he'll be a famous nuclear physicist some-day." Just as I was beginning to believe my own fantasy, the voice of reality broke through. It was Mr. Stevens. Oh yeah, I was still in the lab, the trash can was still smoking, and I was feeling like a complete and utter idiot—an expelled idiot.

Mr. Stevens told us to sit down. Jonathan immediately sat down on the floor (what a dork). Then Mr. Stevens asked, "Does anyone have an explanation for . . . this?" (And he pointed to the smoking garbage can.) At first no one said anything. Jonathan looked like he was going to cry and I wasn't sure my mouth was working, so Bill finally spoke up and tried to explain what we had been "attempt-ing to accomplish." He used as many big words as he could, but Mr. Stevens wasn't buying it. He just stared at us, shak-ing his head. My face was so hot, I was sure I was going to die of heatstroke, if I was lucky. After a while he said something about catching the school on fire, not thinking before we acted, consequences (that word again), and ba-sically told us we had been real stupid and lucky. By this time I was sweatin' all over and I was hoping I would just kinda melt into the floor.

Then, he kinda smiled and said, "You know, guys, I think your enthusiasm is great. Your hearts, if not your heads, are in the right place and since there's no real harm done, except to the garbage can, we can consider the incident closed and forgotten." Then he got serious. "But next time, I won't be so understanding." We looked at each other like dummies. I guess none of us could believe we weren't being hauled down to the office. Mr. Stevens stood up and mumbled something about how when he was a kid he had a few "run-ins with authority" and had made a few "creative mistakes" (whatever that meant).

Suddenly Jonathan started laughing kinda hysterically and couldn't stop. He was turning red and tears were coming out of his eyes. Then Bill started laughing and coughing and choking, so I joined in (laughing, not choking). I guess it was just relief that the school and our pitiful lives hadn't gone up in smoke.

. . .

I wonder if I'll make it to the eighth grade.

30

A Matthews Family Outing

Saturday, December 8

My family is a bunch of dorks. I don't know how I could be related to them.

Bill asked if I could spend the night last weekend. Mom said no, of course. Why should I have a life? She said I had to go on a family outing (oh joy). Then she smiled that wonderful smile of hers and said if I wanted, I could invite a friend to come with us. I called Aaron to see if he wanted to go, but he didn't sound too excited about going on a "family outing." He said he had other plans. So I called Bill back. I didn't know if he would want to come with us either but he said, "Sure thing."

We went ice skating at the new rink at the mall. I've never been ice skating before, but it was a lot like Rollerblading. After a while, Bill and I could skate pretty fast and take the corners with no problem. We even started skating backward a little. Dad skated a lot when he was a kid so he was really good. But Mom? Mom was a pitiful case. She's never ice skated before and she was terrible. She's such a klutz. First she hung onto the sides and every time she let loose, she would fall down. Then Bill and I tried to help by holding her hands and she did pretty good until we let go. Then her arms started flapping like a bird and her feet were spinning out of control, and she ended up flat on her back. So then Chelsea and Wyatt tried to help, but she fell and pulled them down right in front of a big group of people. Mom was laughing so hard she couldn't move out of the way, so everyone had to skate around her. It would've been really embarrassing if I hadn't been on the other side of the rink at the time. She ended up crawling off the ice. She said enough was enough and that she was getting too old for "contact sports."

Since she couldn't skate, she sat on the side and became (oh no!) a cheerleader. Every time Wyatt and Chelsea went all the way around without falling, she would stand up and clap and yell and whistle through her fingers. Every time I tried doing something hard like turning full circles, she would stand up and yell, "That's my son!" (Please, someone, shut her up.) And every time Bill skated past her she would yell, "Go, Bill, go!" I about died of embarrassment.

Bill said he thought it was great. He's kinda weird that way, he thinks Mom is cool. I think he kinda likes her.

Then a couple of girls from school showed up so Bill and I talked to them for a while. I guess we started to show off, you know, doing 360s, little jumps and stuff. We started skating backward real fast and we were yelling at the girls to watch us. They started yelling back at us and we just kept smiling and waving and being so cool, except I guess they were trying to tell us to watch out. But it was too late. Bill and I skated right into a bunch of little kids playing crack-the-whip and flattened them all. It was so humiliating. Kids were crying and slipping and one even hauled off and hit me! We were trying to help but they just kept crying and yelling (and falling). Then all the moms came out and gave us real dirty looks and called us "hooligans" (whatever that means). When all the kids were finally off the ice we looked over at the girls, hoping they hadn't seen the whole mess, but they had and they were laughing their heads off. Then Chelsea skated by and yelled, "Why don't you big kids pick on someone your own size!" Why me? Why always me?

I think Mom and Dad must have felt sorry for us. They took us out for ice cream afterward and never said a word about what happened, although Mom kept chuckling all the way home and tried to cover it up by coughing.

. . .

All in all, it was a typical Matthews family outing. A whole lot of pain for a little bit of pleasure.

31

My Dad . . .
the Pilot

Parents are so strange. Just when you think you know them, just when you have them all figured out, they turn around and surprise you.

This week was career week. Different people came and talked about their jobs and what they had to do to become what they are. One of the guys who came works on the computer programs at NASA. It was so cool. He said something that really made me think: "If you prepare yourselves with the right choices, the right education, and you have the right attitude, you can become anything . . . *anything!*" The way he said "anything" made me feel like I really could do anything. I used to think I wanted to be a race-car driver. Both me and Aaron did, and maybe make horror movies too. But after the gunpowder report in science, I think it would be cool to be a scientist (but not blow anything up). What he said really made me think about school and how I probably should try harder.

But the best part was the part I thought would be the worst—Dad came. About a month ago Mom was helping me clean out my backpack and found the paper asking which parents wanted to come to career week. I meant to throw it away but forgot. She asked if I wanted Dad to come and I said, "That's all right. I know he has a busy schedule. I understand and I don't mind." I didn't want her to think I *didn't* want him to come (but I didn't). I figured he'd be boring or embarrassing. I mean, I like Dad and he's really cool, but around all the kids? I don't think so. But she got all excited, like moms always do, and checked Dad's schedule. When she came out of her bedroom she was all bouncy and bubbly and smiling from ear to ear. "Guess what, Dean? He'll be here that day. Won't that be great!" And she signed the paper and gave it to me to bring back to school. I thought about not giving the paper to the office, but knowing Mom, she would call the school to see why Dad hadn't been asked to talk and then I would be in trouble (again).

Now, I'm glad he came. It was really great. He came dressed in his pilot's uniform and looked so important. All the kids thought he was the best because he sounded so smart but he was funny too. He brought some of the model planes from home (we have about a thousand of them) like the first passenger planes, the TWA Constellation, and the new ones like the 777s and the Airbus. He brought everyone a poster with a cool picture of the space shuttle taking off. It says, "I may be a dreamer, but some day man will fly." (Wilbur Wright said that!)

He talked about all the things we talk about at home, but in front of our class it sounded different—it made a lot more sense. He hardly seemed like my dad. He hardly even looked like my dad. He talked about hard work and persistence and the right choices and preparation and he even threw in a couple jokes that everyone laughed at.

The kids asked him lots of questions and he had real good answers. One girl asked him if he ever got to meet any passengers. He said yes, he got to meet them once in a while. Like one little old lady who wasn't even a passenger on his plane but he remembers real well. He was walking down the terminal after a flight and this old lady stopped him and asked him where Delta Flight 202 was checking in. Since Dad doesn't work for Delta, he said he didn't know and tried to tell her where she could find out. She interrupted him like she hadn't heard him and said, "Young man, just pick up my bags and bring them to where I have to check in for the flight." So he had to say to her again, "Ma'am, I don't know anything about Delta Flight

202. I don't work for Delta. But if you would like your bags taken to the Delta counter, I would be happy to get a skycap to help you." She looked real surprised and said, "Aren't you a skycap? I thought since you were in a blue uniform, you were one of those chaps who takes our bags and makes sure they get on the plane." I guess she didn't see his wings or know that all the stripes on his jacket said he was a pilot and a captain. But instead of getting mad or laughing at her, Dad just got a skycap with one of those neat golf carts people ride in, helped her and her bags into the cart, and told the guy where she needed to be. She thanked him, started digging in her purse and muttering, "Oh dear . . . oh dear . . ." When Dad asked if something was wrong she just said, "Oh no, I was just looking for a quarter so I could give you a little tip. You've been such a nice young man. But all I have is a dime." And then she gave him the dime! We all laughed so hard. Especially at the way Dad's face went when he said "young man" and "a little tip." Everyone told me how they thought he was so cool.

■   ■   ■

I guess I never realized how smart Dad is or what he had to do to become a pilot or everything he does at work. I guess I was never very interested. I think I'm really proud of him.

32

The Best Christmas Ever

Wednesday, December 26

Getting ready for Christmas and wishing for all the great gadgets in the world is almost as good as Christmas morning and all the presents. Mom always tries to remind us that "it's better to give than to receive." (Yeah right, Mom. Get real.) But after this year, I'm thinking maybe she's right. It all started the night before Christmas.

Since one of Señora Ana's daughters is visiting from Mexico, we invited them to spend Christmas Eve with us. Señora Ana said she would make us an extra-special Christmas Eve dinner. Mom said she didn't have to, but Señora

Ana said, "No, no, no. You work very hard, little lady" (she always calls Mom little lady) "and I will help." So she did. It was a very strange Christmas Eve dinner, with all the hot Mexican food. But it was fun.

After dinner, we got to have a piñata. It was in the shape of a Santa Claus. We were blindfolded and took a broom handle and tried to hit the piñata hard enough to break it. Chelsea swung hard, missed completely, and ended up on the floor. When it was my turn, I about creamed Dad. But then when it was Wyatt's turn, he smacked it good, and inside was a whole bunch of candy. Then Señora Ana and her daughter lit some candles and sang some Mexican Christmas songs. They showed us a Mexican dance and even Dad got up and tried it. He looked pretty silly, but we had a really good time. Then Señora Ana and her daughter went to a midnight mass at their church. I never heard of going to church at midnight. It's a good thing we don't go to midnight mass. Dad has a hard enough time staying awake at church and we go at nine o'clock in the morning.

Oh, and of course we had our family tradition—the jammies. Mom has this tradition that's real important to her. Every year she makes us pajamas. It is so humiliating to be dressed up in jammies that match Wyatt and Chelsea's. I've tried to talk to Mom about how I'm just too old for this tradition, but you can't tell Mom anything. After all, this is not a democracy. But I guess it wasn't too bad this year. Instead of regular pajamas, Mom got each of us a big white T-shirt and wrote our name on it in that T-shirt paint she has. Then she gave us a pair of sweatpants. I guess it could have been a lot worse, like the year Mom made us ones that had little red doggies all over them, then took a picture of the three of us and sent it to everyone.

Christmas morning, Wyatt got a big battery-powered car that looks like a jeep, Chelsea got a fancy boom box with a CD player for her room, and . . . I got the remote control airplane I wanted! It is so cool. It's called a Corsair and it was used in World War II. Dad and I took it out Christmas Day for a couple of trial runs. Dad says that soon we'll be able to do tricks with it and maybe join a remote control airplane club. But for now, I'm doing good just to keep the thing in the air. It's not as easy as I thought it was going to be but it's great.

But the most exciting thing wasn't even a present I got. It was the present we gave Señora Ana. She came by Christmas morning to see how we were and have Christmas breakfast with us like she always does. Then Dad told her we had a big surprise and Chelsea piped up, "Close your eyes . . . close your eyes," and started jumping up and down until I wanted to hit her. Señora Ana closed her eyes and held out her hand. Her eyes bugged out when she saw what it was. Dad had bought her a plane ticket to Mexico so she could go home with her daughter to spend a week with the rest of her family—her mother, two sisters, and I think a brother, plus she has another son who lives in Mexico. She hasn't been home to Mexico in ten years. She leaves tomorrow and won't be back until after New Year's.

She was so funny when Dad gave her the ticket. She cried and cried and kept saying *"gracias"* (which means "thank you"). Then she stopped all of a sudden and said, "No, no, no. I can no go!" When Mom said, "Why on earth not?" Señora Ana said, "There will be no one to look after my niños" (that's us). "I no can leave them with a stranger. No, no, no. I can no go!" Mom just laughed and said she was going to take some vacation and would "baby-sit" us until Señora Ana came back home. She promised Señora Ana she would take very good care of us. Señora Ana gave us all a big hug and started crying some more. Then she hugged us some more, saying things in Spanish I didn't understand but they sounded great.

• • •

What a great Christmas! It felt so good when Señora Ana was so happy and she kept crying and hugging us. I like that feeling.

So much for fuzzy feelings. Mom just came in and told me it's time to write thank-you notes. I wonder if I could just get Chelsea to say "thank you from Dean" in her thank-you notes? Oh right. I'm sure she would just love to. She'd just tell Mom and then it'd be back to life as usual around the Matthews's house. You know what would be the absolute best? If Christmas lasted an entire month. And there were no such things as thank-you notes . . . just thank-you hugs!

33

A Career in Politics

Monday, January 7

It all started when Bill nominated me for student council. They wait to elect the four seventh-grade representatives until halfway through the year. I guess they figure us dumb seventh graders need a couple of months to get used to the "big-kid" school. Anyway, Bill nominated me! I couldn't believe it. Then he actually got twenty-five kids to sign my nomination application! Unbelievable! And that's how I ended up in front of the entire school, giving an election speech.

Mom had really helped with my speech (thank goodness). She made me practice and practice and practice, first in front of her, then in front of a mirror, and finally in front of the whole family. I really thought I had it nailed, but when I was sitting up on the stage in front of the whole school, I started feeling sick. I could feel the sweat trickle down my armpits and wondered if I looked as bad as I felt. The girl who talked before me was pretty good. Everything she said sounded intelligent. She made sense. She had memorized the whole thing and she even smiled.

When it was my turn, I got up to the podium and just stared at everyone. It was like I couldn't remember who I was, where I was, or what I was doing up there. Then it hit me . . . oh yeah, student council, Bill's great idea. I went to get my speech cards but I couldn't find them. I could have sworn I had put them in my pants pocket but they weren't there! So I felt all the way to the bottom of my pocket to make sure there wasn't a hole, and as I was digging, people started laughing. I guess I did look pretty pitiful. I checked the other pocket and they weren't there either. I checked both back pockets but no luck and I didn't have any more pockets. By now, it felt like I had been up there for three days. *Everyone* was laughing including Bill and all twenty-five dorks who had signed my nomination application. My face was getting hotter, my chest felt heavy, and I was having a hard time breathing. I could have sworn

I was having a heart attack. Then someone tapped me on the shoulder. I about jumped off the stage! It was Tasha, the girl who had just given her speech. Funny how I could remember her name but not my own. *She* had my cards. She whispered, "They were under your chair." (Oh yeah, that's where I put them so they wouldn't get all wrinkled.) By this time everyone was practically falling out of their seats they were laughing so hard and I figured the whole thing was pretty much a lost cause, so I started my speech by saying, "I really am a lot smarter than I look." That made everyone laugh harder. It took a while for everyone to calm down, but eventually I made it through my speech without too many mistakes.

Then on Friday we had elections and today I found out. . . . I won!

. . .

I still can hardly believe that I actually won the election. I probably won, not because of the things I said or because I was the most qualified, but because everyone remembered "the idiot."

I guess I don't really care why they voted for me. I'm just glad I won. Student council is going to be pretty cool. We're going to talk about school activities and help organize them. We even get to tell the teachers what other kids think about school and why they might not like it and then we try to come up with ideas to make the school better.

I could really get into this political scene. Maybe instead of being a scientist, I should go into politics. Maybe I could become president of the United States. Except then I'll hire someone to give all my speeches.

34

The Date—
Part One

Monday, January 14

There's a Sweetheart Dance coming soon. It's where the girls ask the boys. And . . . I can't believe it. . . . Tasha asked me! I got to go. I have to do homework.

Who am I kidding? I can't do homework right now. I still can't believe this happened. Tasha asked me to the Sweetheart Dance! I don't know about this.

I sorta knew Tasha last year even though we weren't in the same class. I noticed her because she's real pretty and she was in a play. It was one of those stupid ones where they have a villain and everyone is supposed to boo at him, and Tasha was the good guy . . . uh girl . . . woman. The play was kinda stupid, but she was pretty good. Now she's in two of my classes and we've kinda become friends. She also ran for student council and is one of the other seventh-grade representatives. Yep, she's the one who found my speech cards when I was acting like such a dork. Which kinda makes me wonder why she would ask me to the dance . . . pity?

Her hair is to her shoulders and brown and she has real dark brown eyes. She's a little shorter than me (which is very good) and she smiles a lot. But what I like best about her is she really listens when I talk to her. She doesn't giggle or look around for her girlfriends or keep saying, "Oh, for sure . . ." And most important, she doesn't act stupid. She says she wants to be a reporter when she grows up and she likes to write poetry. I don't really like poetry all that much. It always seems like poets take simple things and complicate them so you can't understand them.

Anyway, Tasha knows all about my journal. I didn't mean for her to know. We were talking in English class one day and I was complaining about all the writing we have to do. She said she didn't really mind so I opened my big mouth and said, "Yeah, well you don't have to write in a journal." So then I kinda had to tell her about Mom's brilliant idea— my journal. I've never told anyone about my journal, not even Aaron. I thought everyone would think it was dumb, but she thought it was cool.

Anyway, she came up to me yesterday in class and we

were talking about the teacher and the homework and stuff like that and suddenly she asked if I was going to the dance. I was trying to be real cool so I said, "No way, not me, dances are so stupid." She looked kinda nervous and said, "Oh," and started to walk away. Then all of a sudden she came back and said, "You might think it's dumb, but would you go with me? I mean, we could go as friends and laugh at everyone else."

At first I felt kind of embarrassed. Then I felt stupid for saying dances were stupid. Then I thought, "It might be OK. We're just friends and if we stay in the corner, no one will see me." So I said, "Yeah, sure, why not. Might be fun," like I was so cool and girls asked me out all the time. I knew I should say something else because she was still standing there smiling at me, but I didn't know what to say so I just said, "Well, I guess I'll see ya around. . . . I mean, I gotta sit down . . . over there . . . in my own seat . . . desk." (I'm so smooth and sophisticated. I'm such a dork.)

But that's not the worst of it. When I started to go back to my seat, I bumped into the desk behind me, the books fell off, the desk slipped, and I ended up on the floor, all tangled up in the desk. I just kinda lay there while everyone laughed. I tried to get up but with all the books and the desk . . . well . . . finally Tasha held out her hand to help me up. How embarrassing, but what else could I do? I wasn't having much luck getting up by myself, so I let her help me up. And that's when all the kissing sounds started. My face was so red, my ears were so hot, and everyone kept making kissing sounds until Miss Eames came in and asked what was going on.

. . .

I don't know if this dance thing is such a good idea.

35

The Date—
Part Two

Friday, January 18

*Just got back from the dance, and I still can't believe it.
It was great! (Although at the beginning, I wasn't too sure.)*

First Tasha and her mom came by the house to pick me
up. I tried to get Mom to send Wyatt and Chelsea somewhere . . . like Alaska. But all she did was send them to their
rooms. She didn't even tie them up or lock them in!

Tasha introduced her mother to me and I introduced
Mom to her except I got it all mixed up and called Tasha
"Mom" and Mom "Tasha" and everyone thought it was real
funny. Then she gave me a bootner . . . or something like
that. I'd never heard of it. It's just a little flower you wear

on your jacket. I gave her a flower for her wrist. Mom got it for me. I told her no one else would do it and that she was being old-fashioned, but as it turned out, Mom did the perfect thing. Tasha thought it was "beautiful." (Wow, you never know when moms are going to be right about something.)

Anyway, after we all got our flowers we just kinda stood there. I really didn't know what I should do next. Suddenly Mom said something about the camera (oh no . . . not the camera) and then both moms started taking pictures and they wouldn't stop. They took pictures of us standing together, then sitting together, then me standing and Tasha sitting, then Tasha on the stairs and me at the bottom of the stairs, then us looking at each other (that was *real* embarrassing). After a while, it got so ridiculous we had to laugh. Mothers can be so weird.

Then while Mom was taking "just one more shot" (with my arm around Tasha), Wyatt walked out. Oh no! So I had to introduce him to Tasha and her mom. He acted so sweet and innocent and polite. "Hello. It's very nice to meet you. Do you love Dean and are you going to marry him?" I thought I was going to die! Both mothers were laughing and said, "Isn't he cute." (Yeah, they'll think "cute" when I get through with him.)

After we got to the dance it got much better. I was planning on standing in a dark corner all night so no one would see us, but all the kids from school were there and everyone else had "dates," so it wasn't so bad. No one danced at first (of course) so Tasha and I just talked. She is so easy to talk to. I thought it would be hard to be around a girl all night, but she made it pretty easy. She asked me about my journal again. She said she thought it was a good idea and she wanted to start one. It got kinda embarrassing when she asked, "Do you think you'll write about our date in your journal?" I didn't know what to say, so like the highly intelligent and advanced species I am, I said, "Uh, I dunno." But really, I like that she asked *me* questions and didn't do all the talking like other girls. It made it easier to be with her and treat her like a normal person.

Finally, the thing I had really been dreading happened. She said, "Well, maybe we should dance." Oh man, I wasn't sure what I looked like when I danced. I sometimes dance at home in my room in front of my mirror and that's pretty sad. But it turned out to be OK. She just started dancing, and I tried to dance like her. Then Bill came over and danced next to us and we had a great time making fun of everyone else. Bill came with Adrianne (my friend from fifth grade) and they looked real good together. Bill is so tall and blond and Adrianne is short as me and she has black hair that hangs all the way down to her waist. Bill says she's fun to be with and makes him laugh. We all hung around together for the rest of the dance and when Tasha's mom came to take us home, she said Bill and Adrianne could come too. She's a cool lady—she even took us all out for ice cream.

When we got to my house, Tasha walked me to the door. That's when I started getting scared again. I mean, what was I supposed to do now? Kiss her, shake her hand, run like a scared rabbit? But it was OK. Tasha said, "I had a really good time and I'm glad you went with me. You're a good friend, Dean Matthews," and she gave me a little hug and walked off. I just stood there feeling kinda stupid since I didn't even hug her back. But I also felt kinda good and all warm inside. She kept waving until her car was way down the street.

I was still feeling pretty good when I called to see why Aaron didn't go to the dance. He said because Stach had gone to a lot of school dances and said they were boring and dumb and only for the little kids. I told him he should've come because it turned out pretty cool.

Then Aaron asked if I wanted to spend the night next weekend. I don't think Mom is going to say yes, but Aaron said he'd have his mom call and ask. He said his mom likes me to come over to their house.

I guess we'll see. I kinda hope I can go. I haven't been over there in a long time. Maybe Mom will be cool about it.

36

Consequences

Saturday, January 26

I am so scared!!! Why when everything is going so good does something so bad have to happen? Mom says I let it happen. I tried to tell her it wasn't my fault! I think I'm in real, real big-time trouble . . . the worst ever! Mom and Dad haven't said anything yet about what happened, but it's only a matter of time.

I went over to Aaron's house to spend the night. I couldn't believe Mom let me, but Aaron's mom called and said everything would be OK. We were out front playing basketball when Stach came over. Stach started bragging about how much fun it was to drive a car. He only has his learner's permit but I guess his mom lets him drive the car sometimes. He asked if we wanted to go for a ride. He said his mom was out on a date so she would never know. Aaron told him we couldn't go out of the yard, but Stach promised we would just go around the block and be right back, "and no one will know, so no one will get mad. It's just a little ride around the block. We're not going to do anything bad and we'll be back before anyone knows we're gone." Then he said something like, "If parents would only loosen up, kids would get along with them much better." At the time, it kinda made sense. But then again, I'm a complete idiot. Anyway, we got in the car.

After going around the block two times (with no one noticing we were gone), Stach asked if we wanted to go downtown where everyone else was driving around. He *promised* we would be right back. Since it was only seven o'clock and Aaron and I didn't have to be in the house until eight thirty, we thought it would be OK. We figured if Aaron's parents asked, we could just say we had taken a long walk to talk. Maybe they would believe that.

We went downtown and drove all around, yelling at people on the sidewalk and other kids on the street. Then a kid drove up and yelled, "Hey, Stach, what kind of car is that? Your mommy's?" And he took off laughing. So Stach took off after him, swearing the whole way.

We went out on a road in the foothills just outside of town where a lot of kids race their cars (even though it's illegal).

When we got there, a whole bunch of kids were hanging around so we parked. Stach said something about "teaching that punk a lesson" and went looking for him. By the time we caught up to him, he was chuggin' a beer with the guy. There was lots of beer everywhere and everyone was smoking and other stuff. Stach asked if we wanted a drink. Aaron said, "Yeah!" and started chuggin' it. I didn't really want any, but I grabbed a can of beer and took a couple of sips. I figured I could just hold it like I was drinking and then no one would make fun of me. Stach and Aaron had a contest to see who could drink a can of beer the fastest. They did it a couple of times and Stach won every time. Boy, can he drink a lot of beer! Then they started spraying beer at each other and me. I got drenched. (I can't stand the smell of beer.)

Finally Stach said it was time to "put up or shut up," which meant it was time to race. I told Aaron that maybe we shouldn't ride in the car while they were racing. So Stach said, "Yeah, maybe you *babies* shouldn't be in the car." Aaron said, "I'm going whether you are or not." Then Stach said, "Run along now, little boy. Go home to your mommy where you belong." Then everyone started making chicken noises, so I decided I would go too (real smooth move).

Aaron hurried and got in the front seat, so I had to sit in back. We got out on the road, side by side with the other car. Stach and the other driver were revving up their engines, everyone was screaming and I was sweatin'. It was getting pretty intense. Just when we were ready to take off, a whole bunch of cops showed up and told everyone to stay where they were. Some of the kids stopped, but others started running. While the cops were trying to chase everyone, Stach hit the gas and took off and (surprise, surprise), the cops chased us. Just like on TV except a lot scarier.

Stach kept going faster and faster, and started swerving every time we went around a curve in the road. I was getting pretty scared and yelled at him to stop. He yelled, "No way! If they catch us, we'll all go to jail!" So I yelled back, "But you said they never do anything to kids." He told me to shut up and kept going faster and faster. Probably the only smart thing I did all night was to put my seat belt on. I yelled at Aaron that he better put his on too. I think he must have been pretty scared because he didn't say anything, he just turned to look at me with a weird look on his face and put his seat belt on.

It was terrible! Cops chasing us, the car swerving all over the place, Stach swearing. Then, when we were going around a real tight curve, Stach lost control of the car. We hit some dirt and gravel and we slid to the other side of the road. I'm not real sure what happened next because it happened way too fast (and I was way too scared), but we ended up crashing through a wooden fence and stopping real hard on the other side of the road facing backward.

Then the cops came . . . three of them. And boy were they

pissed. They yelled, "Get your hands on the dashboard!" Then they shouted, **"NOW!"** I didn't know where to put my hands since I was in the backseat and couldn't reach the dashboard so I put my hands on my head. It seemed the logical thing to do (yeah right . . . *now* I'm using my head).

By this time there was one cop on the passenger side of the car, one on the driver's side, and one right in front of us. The one in front was as big as a house and he had his gun out! I thought I was going to die! All of a sudden, Stach opened his door like he was going to run for it. The cop in front cocked his gun and yelled, "Hold it!" Then he told us to "get out of the car real slow." When I got out my legs were shaking so bad I could hardly stand. Aaron almost fell out and finally Stach got out of the car. One of the cops said, "They're just little kids." (That made me feel real good.) They told us to face the car and put our hands on the hood (just like in the movies) and two of the cops checked us for weapons. I couldn't believe this was happening to me! The one with the gun finally put it away, so at least I didn't have to worry about being shot (at least not yet), and asked if we were all OK (oh yeah, except for heart failure and terminal stupidity). As it turned out Stach had a cut on his lip and said his back hurt and he was still swearing and moaning and acting kind of weird. I heard one of the cops say he was going to call the paramedics. Then the big one said, "You can turn around, boys, but stand right there against the car." The one with the mustache started checking inside the car and guess what he found? Beer under the driver's seat (as if things weren't bad enough).

While he was checking, the other cop asked us our names. Aaron and I told him, except I had to repeat it twice because when I tried to tell him the first time, no sound came out. Then the cop asked Stach his name, but Stach wouldn't tell. The cop asked him for some I.D., and that's when it hit the fan! Stach called him a pig and shoved him! They had him facedown on the ground with cuffs on before I could breathe. He kept swearing and trying to fight them and they kept telling him to calm down. It was pretty bad. They finally got him sitting up against the car.

Finally after about two centuries, the paramedics got there. They checked us and I guess Aaron and I were OK, but Stach was acting super strange by this time, banging his head against the car, spitting at the cops' shoes, and muttering to himself, so the paramedics said they should take him to the hospital. The cops asked him again what his name was: "It is very important for you to cooperate so we can get you proper medical attention and contact your parents." He just kept shouting things like, "Go ahead . . . see if I care . . . see if they care . . . you can all go to h— ." Then he got sick and threw up all over one of the cops.

The cop in the patrol car finally came up and said, "This car belongs to a woman named Angela Calabrese. It looks like we've got a stolen car here, boys." I felt like someone had just punched all the wind out of me, but Aaron spoke up and said, "Angela Calabrese is Stach's mom," and then he told the cops Stach's name and address. That's when Stach lost it completely. He cussed at Aaron and said he was going to kill him. He swore at me and said I better watch out too. He said it was all our fault he had gotten caught and we were going to be sorry we were ever born. Then he started swearing at the cops again and told them he didn't care about anything! It got pretty bad.

The paramedics finally got Stach strapped to one of their funny cots and took him to the hospital. Then they handcuffed me and Aaron and took us to the police station in separate cars. That was so scary, sitting in the backseat behind the cage. My wrists hurt and I couldn't sit all the way back because they had handcuffed us with our hands behind our backs, so when we would turn a corner it was hard to keep my balance and I kept falling over. I was not having a good time.

When we got to the police station, they took me to a room, took the handcuffs off and said I'd have to wait. Then they left and locked me in. I have never felt so sick and so scared and so *stupid*. The room was small and a yucky yellow color. It looked like it hadn't been painted in fifty years. And believe it or not, there was a mirror in the room, and I knew, just like on TV, it was a two-way mirror. That made me real nervous, wondering who was on the other side looking at me and talking about me, deciding how long I would have to go to jail. But something I didn't know from

TV is that the chairs and table in the room are bolted to the floor. I guess so you couldn't throw them at the cops or something. I don't know. I can't imagine anyone thinking he could get away with hitting a cop in the middle of a cop shop with a million people watching you from behind the two-way mirror.

I think that had to be just about the scaredest I've ever been (or ever want to be). But then it got even worse. My parents showed up! They came in with one of the cops who had picked us up and another lady. Mom and Dad said the cops were going to ask some questions and I was to answer them truthfully. Then the cops read me my rights and I had to sign a paper that said the cops read me my rights and that someone was there with me (namely my parents) and that I was talking of my own free will. My hand was shaking so bad I don't think anyone will be able to read my name.

Then the cop asked what had gone on . . . if I had been drinking or taking drugs . . . how old I was . . . about Stach and Aaron . . . and a whole lot more questions. No one was smiling, no one was being understanding. The cop would even yell once in a while and everyone looked way too serious. Then he asked me if I knew how much trouble I was in. I started to tell everyone it wasn't my fault and that I didn't do anything wrong. I wasn't drinking beer, I wasn't the one driving, or doing anything. Then the cop got nasty, "You didn't have *anything* to drink?" I said, "Just a sip." And he said, "It smells like a lot more than a sip, and that's illegal consumption." Then he asked if we had permission to use the car, and I said I didn't know, and he asked it again. "Did you have permission to take the car?" I said, "No," and he said there were a couple of laws that went along with that, grand theft auto for a start. So I said, "But it wasn't me. It was Stach." And the cop said, "You were a willing participant in several illegal acts and that makes you, at the very least, an accomplice." Then he added, "If I were you, I wouldn't worry so much about Stach. I'd start worrying about yourself because you're in a world of hurt." I looked at Mom and Dad. Dad had a serious look on his face and wouldn't look at me, and Mom looked like she was going to cry, but she didn't say anything. I felt like throwing up . . . then dying.

Then the cop started asking questions about Stach. Did I know he had been drinking (yes), did I know he took the car without permission (kinda), did I know he had been taking drugs (WHAT?! Oh great, what next?)

Finally they told me I could go into a waiting area while they did some paperwork and talked to my parents. When I got there, Aaron was kinda slouched on the bench and he looked like he had been crying. He said his parents were still talking to the cops. When they finally came out, his mom was crying pretty hard and his dad started yelling at him before they even got out of the police station. I guess he's in a lot more trouble than even me. His dad yelled something about drinking . . . *again* . . . and being with

Stach and honesty and trust and *car theft!* Then Mom and Dad came out. They signed some papers, asked me again if I was OK, then Mom hugged me (?) and said we should go home.

.   .   .

They didn't say anything all the way home, but I know they've got to be really mad. When Mom's face looks like that and Dad's jaw twitches, I know I'm in real big trouble. And I don't think I'm going to be able to talk my way out of it this time.

How did all this happen?

37

More Fallout

Sunday, January 27

Well, they finally started yelling!! I was starting to think they wouldn't say anything since I really didn't do anything so wrong and I had to go through that whole criminal scene at the police station, but no such luck.

They brought me into their room and it was real quiet, so I decided to try to be funny and said, "I guess you're wondering why I've called you all together." Mom shook her head and Dad told me I was in too much trouble to try to be a smart aleck. Then it started.

First Dad said, "What on earth were you thinking?" Then Mom said before I could answer, "Thinking? That's his problem, he doesn't think. He just goes off and does whatever his friends tell him to do." Then Dad said, "Do you realize exactly what happened? Do you have any idea what you did?" I said, "Yes." Then he yelled, "No you don't! You don't have *any* idea!" I just sat there thinking how much I hate it when they both start screaming at me. I don't understand half of what they're saying, they never take a breath so how am I supposed to answer their questions, and they get so wound up they are totally unreasonable.

When they finally slowed down, I tried to explain, "I didn't drink anything except one little sip of beer. The reason I smelled like beer was because someone spilled some on me." (That sounded lame even to me.) "I didn't mean to get into trouble. It wasn't even my idea." I kept telling them *it wasn't my fault!*

Then Mom asked me, "Who forced you to get in the car? There's absolutely no one you can blame for the trouble you're in except you." Then she picked up speed. "Did you know how much Aaron and Stach had been drinking? Did you know drugs were found on Stach? Were you using drugs? Did you use your head at any time during the evening?" I tried to tell her that Stach and Aaron might have done all that bad stuff, BUT I HADN'T!

Mom took a deep breath. I thought she was going to start yelling again, but she started to cry. Then Dad said in a real low voice, "You know something, son? It's pure dumb luck you're not dead. I still can't believe that someone as smart as you would do something so dumb and dangerous as get in a car with a driver who has been drinking."

Then it finally hit me, I mean why Mom and Dad were so mad. *They were scared!* They were thinking about what *could have* happened to me. That got me thinking about how fast Stach had been going, how we skidded and crashed, and how it could have been worse, *a lot* worse.

Dad said I was going to have to appear before a judge because I was in the same car as Stach and Aaron. They're in more trouble than me because I guess they already have stuff on police records. But I'm still in plenty of trouble.

. . .

How did this all happen? I tried to tell Mom and Dad I was sorry. Dad wouldn't listen. He just walked out of the room. Mom was still kind of crying and told me to go to my room. I feel so bad and scared. This is the worst I've ever felt. Then again, I guess this is about the worst thing I've ever done.

I wonder if everyone at school will know what happened? I wonder if I'll be kicked out of student council? I wonder if Bill and Tasha will still be my friends? I wonder if Mom and Dad will ever forgive me? I wonder if things will ever be like they used to be—simple.

38

The Whole Story

Sunday, February 3

Dad is still so mad and quiet. I can't even talk to him. I didn't think I was in that much trouble. Mom started treating me normal, but I can't figure out Dad. Maybe he doesn't want anything to do with me ever again.

I finally got the nerve to ask Mom why Dad was acting so strange. At first she didn't say anything, then she had me come into her room. She got in her little desk and pulled out a scrapbook. She found an old piece of newspaper and told me to read it. It was about two kids, one of whom had borrowed his dad's car for a ride. I was tired of lectures so I told her, "I learned my lesson. I don't need to read about other kids who got in the same kind of trouble." She got real mad and told me if I cared about making things right with Dad, I better read it.

It was about these two kids who decided to see how fast the car could go up a canyon road. On a sharp turn, the kid driving lost control of the car and hit the side of the mountain. They swung around and fell over the side of the hill. The passenger was killed. The driver was paralyzed. The police found out the driver had been drinking. They didn't say if the other boy had been drinking or not. While I was reading, it all started sounding kinda familiar, and not because the same thing had almost happened to me, but something else. Anyway, I told Mom I understood what can happen when you get into a car with someone who's been drinking. Then Mom told me to finish the article, where they mentioned the names of the boys who were involved. The passenger, the kid who had been killed in the car, was DEAN MATTHEWS!

At first it didn't sink in. I couldn't figure out why my name was in the paper. And then it hit me. This Dean was my uncle Dean, the one who died when dad was just thirteen. The one I had been named after. I couldn't believe it! I looked at Mom but I didn't know what to say. She sat down beside me and told me the whole story. She said that all his life Dad had really looked up to his big brother, tagged along after him kinda like Wyatt does to me, and had really loved him. She said Uncle Dean was a really cool big brother. He let Dad go everywhere with him, like movies and camping and stuff. She said when his brother died, it really messed Dad up. And he didn't get over it for a long time. She said Dad still can't talk about his brother without crying. He really misses him and that's why I was named after him.

Mom said, "Your dad's brother had a lot of potential. He was smart and good-looking and a super athlete. He probably could have gotten scholarships for both football and basketball. And everyone liked him. He was such a great kid. He didn't drink or do drugs or anything like that. But that night he let his friend do his thinking for him and he paid for it with his life." She said when they got the call from the cops telling them I had been in an accident and who I was with, Dad got so scared—more scared than Mom's ever seen him, and that he totally blew the speed limit getting to the cop shop. She said she saw tears! And that's why he still looks so mad . . . because he was so scared, because it brought up all the old bad memories. She said he kept saying the same thing the whole way to the police station, "Not again."

. . .

I guess I didn't think about all this stuff. I didn't think we would get in any trouble. I didn't think Stach would be so stupid. I never thought anyone could really get hurt. Mom's right, I didn't think at all. I can't believe how stupid, stupid, stupid I was . . . I am.

I wonder if Dad will ever talk to me again. I wonder if I've really ruined everything. I wonder if Dad hates me. What am I going to do?

39

The Dust Settles

Friday, February 15

Everyone at school is OK. At least, no one said much. Most kids didn't know anything since they don't read the newspaper. And the kids that did know about it just asked me if I was all right. I had to go to the vice principal's office and got warned and lectured about what happened. But they said after talking to the cops and to Mom and thinking it over, I still get to be on the student council, if I "keep my nose clean." (Adults have such strange expressions.)

Aaron didn't come to school all week because he's got a sore neck and a black eye where he hit the dashboard. I guess the doctor says he's OK. I tried to call but his mom said he doesn't want to talk to anybody, not even me. Their family is going to "family counseling" and Aaron has probation for a year because of this and a couple of other things I didn't even know about. Mrs. Timmons says she's really sorry. Me too.

Stach is in juvenile detention for at least two years, maybe more if he doesn't clean up his act. Mom said he was charged with destruction of property, joyriding, illegal consumption, endangerment, possession of drugs and alcohol, and assaulting a police officer! I bet his mom is really mad this time. Mom said, "No, his mom is probably just real sad."

40

Court

Wednesday, February 20

You hear on TV about guys who are career criminals. They must be nuts! I don't even like being a one-time criminal. It's the pits!

We went to court today, me and Mom. Even though it was scary, it was kind of interesting. It wasn't like on TV. Mom and I were in a room alone with a judge. He said that he had already talked to Mom and Dad, the cops, the school, the prosecuting attorney, and another lawyer who's a friend of Mom and Dad's, and after all that, he decided we could keep it simple, which meant I didn't have to have a trial or anything like that.

The judge said it seemed like I was in the wrong place at the wrong time with the *wrong people!* He said I was being charged with illegal consumption and asked me how I pled. I looked at Mom. We had talked about all this, about what to expect, so I said, "Guilty." Then I hurried and said, "Your Honor." The judge kinda smiled at that but then he got serious again. He gave me a lecture and told me that there were a lot of bad consequences that could happen if I kept doing things like this. He talked about jail and choices and ruining my life. I could feel my neck and face getting hotter and hotter. Then he said, "Young man, after reviewing your case and your school record, the best thing I can do for you is give you one hundred hours of community service."

All I could do was stare at him. I couldn't believe I wasn't going to jail. But I was going to do . . . what?? He explained that community service would be doing stuff like washing cop cars or cleaning at the courthouse (he mentioned bathrooms). But that wasn't all. He also sentenced me to write a five-hundred-word essay on the dangers of alcohol. (All adults must read the same books about kids and discipline.) He also said he would be getting a report from the school on me every three months for a whole year. Then he said, "I'm being nice to you this time, but next time don't count on it." Then he said I was dismissed and he never wanted to see me again. He won't.

When we walked out of the courthouse, my legs felt rubbery and weak, but other than that I actually felt pretty good. Mom put her arm around me and hugged me and told me how glad she was that I was all right. Then, without me even knowing it was going to happen, I started crying! Here I am, almost thirteen years old and I was crying like a baby. And once I started I couldn't stop. It was so weird.

When we got in the car, I told Mom how sorry I really was. I told her how sad I was that Aaron and I weren't best friends anymore. I promised her I would *never* make such a stupid mistake again and that I really wanted her to trust me. I told her I was sorry I had scared her and Dad and I really meant all of it. Then Mom started to cry too! There we were, sitting in a car in front of the courthouse crying. People walking by probably thought we were a couple of crazies but the really funny thing about it was, I didn't even care.

We both finally stopped crying and I felt a lot better. Mom said she did too. I asked her if Dad would ever be able to trust me again. She said, "You'll have to earn his trust. It's all up to you." Then she told me she loved me (like she always does), "and your dad does too."

I don't know. He doesn't act like it. I hope she's right.

41

Making It Right

Sunday, February 24

Dad won't talk to me. He won't even look at me. I've ruined everything!

It's hard to talk to someone who won't even look at you but I've decided Dad and I need to talk. Or at least, I need to talk to Dad and apologize for being the world's stupidest son.

Dad was working in his bedroom last night. I really wanted to talk to him, but I just knew he was going to say he would never trust me ever again and that he didn't care what I did—just to leave him alone. Finally, I got some courage and decided to try to talk to him. When I walked into his room, he was working at the desk. He wouldn't even look at me and I almost walked right back out. But then he asked if I wanted something. I took a deep breath and said, "I'm really sorry I disappointed you and I won't ever do it again." I sounded so stupid. He still didn't look at me but said, "Well, it's over. Let's forget about it."

I felt so bad. I felt like walking out and running away. But then I decided to tell him I knew all about his brother and the accident and everything. I told him I was real sorry Uncle Dean had died and how double sorry I was that I had scared him so bad. I told him I knew I had made some really dumb choices and that my problems were all *my* fault and no one else's. I finally said, "I know I'm stupid sometimes, but I'll try really hard never to be stupid ever again." That made him kind of laugh and he looked at me (finally) and he had tears in his eyes! He got up and walked over to me and kinda grabbed me and gave me a big, tight hug. He hasn't hugged me since I was a little kid (mainly because I didn't want him to, I guess). But all of a sudden, it felt really good to be hugging my dad.

Then, in kind of a funny, scratchy voice, Dad said, "You know, son, I'm very proud of you, and I will always love you, even when you do dumb things. It's just that when I look at you, I see greatness. I know you're going to grow up and do something really special and I just want to make sure you have that chance." He hugged me for a long time and guess what? I started crying again. Then he sat down on the edge of the bed and wiped his eyes with the back of his hand and I wiped my eyes and my nose.

. . .

I guess we're OK now because he asked if I was up to the challenge of a video game. I let him win . . . this one time.

42

Alternative Solutions

Aaron's been suspended from school! I can't believe it. After everything we've been through . . . I just can't believe it.

He got caught smoking and spray painting the walls in the boys' bathroom. He's been suspended for a week. I don't know what good that's going to do. He'll probably just get into more trouble if he doesn't have to go to school. He'll hang out at the mall since his parents work, or sit around the house and watch TV. Like that will help anything. I don't think it's the best thing to do to kids who get into trouble. It doesn't solve anything. Maybe I should say something at student council. Nah. They'll just say it's none of my business. And besides, who would listen to me? I've been in trouble too.

I was talking to Mom about Aaron getting suspended from school and how dumb I thought it was. I told her I felt like telling the teachers and the principal that it doesn't do any good and it doesn't work. Mom said, "So, why don't you?" Just like that she says, "Why don't you?" I said, "Yeah right. Like they care what I think." Then she said, "If you think it's wrong and doesn't work, you should tell them. Your opinion is just as important as anyone else's and maybe you see things from a better point of view. What have you got to lose?"

I thought about that and came to an interesting conclusion. She might be right. (I have a pretty smart mom.) But then she complicated everything. She asked if I had a better answer for the problem. "You know, lots of people complain about things, but not many do anything about them. So why don't you think about it and come up with a couple of alternative solutions?" (Mom loves big words.) Then she said if I still felt strongly about the whole thing, I should go to the student council with my ideas. She said the worst that could happen is they would say, "Thanks, but no thanks . . ." and the best that could happen is I could make a difference. I wonder if a short, skinny seventh grader can really make a difference?

Anyway, the other night Tasha, Bill, and Adrianne were

over at the house playing video games and I was telling them about what Mom said about opinions and alternative solutions. They all said they agreed with her and me. In fact, we all got so excited talking about it, we stopped playing video games and started writing down some of our ideas. Mom let everyone stay for dinner so we could keep working. We finally came up with four really good ideas. We all decided Tasha should write them in a report (since she's the best writer and speller). Then they decided *I* should be the one to present it to the student council. That's right. Me . . . Mr. Super Speaker.

．　．　．

Actually, this is kind of exciting but I'm nervous. Tasha said, "You'll do a great job. Remember your election speech?" (How can I ever forget?) Mom keeps saying she knows I'll do great because I believe in what I'm doing. Dad says he's really proud of me and my friends and he knows I'll do just fine. I hope he's right.

43

Different Paths

Sunday, March 10

I just got off the phone with Aaron's dad. I can't believe what's happened!

I haven't seen much of Aaron. Not since we got in the accident and his suspension and everything. Anyway, I guess he snuck out of the house last night and went to a party with a bunch of high school kids. The kids were passing around all kinds of pills and booze and stuff, and I guess Aaron tried just about everything they gave him. He got real sick and passed out. One of the girls at the party thought he looked pretty bad and said they should take him home. When they couldn't wake him up, they got scared and called his dad. They ended up taking him to the hospital. They had to pump his stomach and he didn't wake up for a long time. Mr. Timmons said Aaron doesn't want to see or talk to anyone (including me), but he thought I would want to know.

I just read our report for the student council again, and I was thinking no matter what happens with the report, it won't help Aaron very much. I can't believe everything that's happened to him . . . to us. We used to do everything together. We used to have so much fun. We were going to be best friends forever. I guess we'll never make that movie about the haunted Ferris wheel. I wish things were different . . . but they're not. I feel terrible.

44

Making a Difference

Wednesday, March 20

Life is getting better . . . I think. At least I'm feeling better, like I'm back in control.

We had student council today. The principal and two vice principals came and sat in the front row with the teacher advisors. I was so scared. I started feeling a little dizzy, but then I looked at Tasha and she smiled and nodded her head. So I took a deep breath, pulled out our report, and started. Even when my voice squeaked, I kept going.

"Principal Fallon, Teachers, Advisors, and Fellow Student Council Representatives. I am speaking on behalf of several students who have observed that the punishment of suspension is counterproductive and rarely works. As a result, we have come up with several alternative solutions for your consideration." (I told you Tasha could write good!) Then I listed our alternative solutions. I kept looking at the principal and vice principals, but I couldn't tell what they were thinking.

Our first idea was that there could be different classes for the kids who were troublemakers. That way, they wouldn't disrupt the other classes, but they would stay in school. We said they would have to get tough but fair teachers for a class like that, but if they could get a teacher who used to be a troublemaker (like our science teacher, Mr. Stevens), it might work real good, because a teacher like that would understand.

Our second idea was that they could make the kids who get into trouble help around the school, like help the janitor or help in the office or help the grounds crew (I got that idea from the community service I have to do every Saturday).

Our third idea came from Mom. She said just because kids get into trouble doesn't mean they're dumb. So I thought it might be a good idea to make some of the kids teachers' aides or they could tutor at the elementary school, like helping the first graders read or the third graders do multiplication and things like that. Or maybe, if they were good at something like sports or art, they could teach classes for the city. Of course a supervisor would still have to be in the class, but if the kids had to keep discipline, maybe they would see how hard it is and they would start to respect the teachers and school more. And maybe if they ended up being good teachers they would feel like they could do something besides get into trouble.

Our last idea was Bill and Adrianne's idea. They said instead of the vice principal always deciding what happens to the kids, maybe there should be a student court. But not like the one the ninth graders have where one kid will take another one to court for something stupid like whose fault it was a book got dropped in the mud. But have a real court (Dad says it's called a "review board"). Then they would listen to what the kid did, listen to *everyone's* side of the story (including the kid who's in trouble) and then help decide how it should be handled.

When I was done I felt like I had just run around the track two hundred times. I was out of breath, my legs were shaking pretty bad, and the sweat was pouring down my sides. Then all the kids started clapping! I was so surprised. When I looked over to the teachers, they were clapping too! I sat down by Tasha and decided no matter how it all turned out, I felt great. Finally the principal stood up and said some of our ideas had "merit" (I think that meant he liked them). Then he said he wanted to meet with me and Tasha and maybe a couple of other kids to work on the ideas, like a committee. He said, "If some of the details could be worked out, we might be willing to try your ideas. Good job, young people. We're proud of you." Then he added, "I'm very impressed with the work you've put into this whole idea. Please plan on presenting it to the school board at their next meeting." I almost fainted, but Tasha was bouncing up and down and poking me in the ribs and whispering, "All right!"

Later when I told Dad, he said, "I'm not surprised in the least. I always knew you had a good head on your shoulders, even if you do misplace it from time to time." (Sounds like a dad, doesn't it.)

• • •

Oh, I almost forgot (yeah right). After the meeting, Tasha gave me another hug, and I stood there like a dummy . . . again. I'm sure she was just real excited about everyone clapping and liking our ideas. But it still felt real nice.

45

Year's End

For the first time in a long time, I don't know what to write. Not much has happened lately.

I finally finished my 500-word essay on alcohol for the judge. Actually it turned out to be 621 words and I have to admit, I learned a lot. But I hope I don't have to do a paper like that ever again.

I've been working Saturday mornings at the courthouse, cleaning windows and floors (and toilets) and washing cop cars. Actually, it's not too bad (except for the toilets).

We've had one meeting with the student council advisors to "firm up our ideas" (that's what Mrs. Shockley calls it), and get ready for the school board meeting. They made me chairman of the committee because the whole thing was originally my idea.

I guess Aaron is going to be OK. He's going to a private school in town. I hope he'll be all right. He still doesn't want to talk to me.

My birthday's almost here and I'm going to be 13. I don't know, when I think back on this year, sometimes I feel 113! I'm exhausted!

Hey! I just realized something. It's been one year since I started writing in my journal. I sure have written a lot. More than I thought I could ever write. Funny how it's not so hard to write in my journal anymore. I just sit down and the words just kind of fall out of my head onto the paper. It's still not my idea of a good time, but it's not so bad.

I read back through some of it and can't believe everything that's happened this year. Mom says it's like a history of me and my family and friends. I still don't think I write very good, not like Tasha. But Mom says she thinks our experiment was a success. As I remember it, it wasn't "our" experiment, it was hers.

Mom also said the most important thing about writing in a journal isn't to make you a good writer, it's to make you a good listener. And she tapped me on my chest, right over my heart. I think I know what she meant, but she makes it so complicated . . . just like a mom.

Just one more entry and my year will be up.

46

The End?

Birthdays are definitely the best day of the whole year.

Mom had a big birthday dinner for me and invited Bill, Adrianne, and Tasha (plus the whole family, of course). We had my favorite dinner—steak, potatoes, and salad. Actually, just steak is my favorite, but Mom says you can't have just meat for a meal—even a birthday meal.

Señora Ana gave me a book on Abraham Lincoln. She says she gave it to me because I'm like Abraham Lincoln, I always tell the truth even when I'm in trouble. I tried to tell her that was George Washington, but she just smiled and told me to read it anyway.

Bill and Adrianne gave me a new controller for my video game, a really cool one.

Chelsea and Wyatt gave me a book of my favorite cartoon character.

Mom gave me . . . nope, not underwear, not a tie, not even a book. She gave me my own phone! Unfortunately, it doesn't come with my own phone number. Just a phone to plug into the jack in my room. When I asked her about my own number, she just smiled that frustrating smile and said, "We'll see when you have a job and can pay the monthly bill."

Even Tasha gave me a present. That was kinda embarrassing, but hey, presents are presents. It was in a huge box and I thought, "Oh no, she's giving me one of those big stuffed animals that girls like, so they think boys like them too." But inside was just a lot of newspaper. It didn't seem like anything else was in there and I was starting to think it was all a joke when she reached in and got a little box. Inside was a tiny flashlight on a long chain. I was confused and I guess it showed so she said, "You can wear it around your neck. It's for the next time you get locked in your locker." (What?!) Then she went on, "I know I never told you, but I was the one who tried to help you get out of your locker the first day of school."

How embarrassing . . . and how amazing! Even after the locker incident and the speech mess and, well, everything else, she still likes me. That's pretty cool.

My best present was the one Dad gave me. He gave me a jacket that belonged to Uncle Dean. It's the one I found in his closet—the blue and gold one. It's way too big for me, but I really like it. Dad says it was his brother's "letterman" jacket for all the sports he played. (No wonder he flipped out when I was trying it on that one time.) He hugged me when he gave it to me and said, "This jacket used to belong to a very special young man and now it belongs to another special young man." For a minute, I thought we might both start crying and totally humiliate ourselves in front of everyone, but then he dug his fingers into my sides and messed up my hair and said, "You better take good care of it or I'll hang you up by your thumbs!"

I got lots of money too. Fifty dollars total. I have to save half (of course) and I've already spent the other half. I bought one of Bill's old video games for ten dollars. Then I bought Tasha an ice cream cone when I walked her home after the party. I got back kinda late since I had a few things to do on the way, so Mom asked if I had any of my birthday money left or if it had "burned a hole through my pocket."

At first, I didn't want to tell her what I bought with the last ten dollars. I knew she'd make a big fuss and say something like, "Oh, and whose idea was that?" Dad said, "Come on, sport, let's see what you blew your money on."

So I had to show them and what did Mom do? She hugged me and started crying!

. . .

Moms are so weird. After all . . . it's only a new journal.